PRAISE FOR P. W. CATAN[ESE]

The Thief and t[he]

"This is the rare fairy tale variant that w... a princess nor romance in sight—and the plot brims with perilous battles, narrow escapes and truly icky elements. . . . Fans of Tim Burton's movies will enjoy this, and will likely welcome Catanese's second adventure, *The Brave Apprentice.*" —*Publishers Weekly*

"A fast-paced, accessible entry in the burgeoning genre of novels based on fairy tales." —*School Library Journal*

The Brave Apprentice

"A charming riff on *The Brave Little Tailor.*" —KLIATT

"Fans of fairy-tale-styled novels like Donna Jo Napoli's *Crazy Jack* (Delacorte, 1999) and *The Prince of the Pond* (Puffin, 1994) will enjoy this story." —*School Library Journal*

"Readers will enjoy the ride." —*VOYA*

The Eye of the Warlock

"Catanese does a great job creating his own believable world rooted within a classic. This is a great middle to high school read, as it shows a wonderful emotional journey and character growth."
—Children's Literature

The Mirror's Tale

"In this accessible entry in the series, Catanese imagines events many years after 'Snow White and the Seven Dwarfs' ends. . . . Buy where there is a demand for fast-paced, easily read adventure fantasy."
—*School Library Journal*

"A wonderful reframing of a classic fairy tale that gives a masculine slant to a story that is often seen as only for girls."
—JustforKidsBooks.com

P. W. CATANESE'S
FURTHER TALES ADVENTURES:

THE THIEF AND THE BEANSTALK

✳

THE BRAVE APPRENTICE

✳

THE EYE OF THE WARLOCK

✳

THE MIRROR'S TALE

The Riddle
of the Gnome

A FURTHER TALES ADVENTURE

P. W. CATANESE

ALADDIN PAPERBACKS
NEW YORK　　LONDON　　TORONTO　　SYDNEY

This book is a work of fiction. Any references to historical events,
real people, or real locales are used fictitiously.
Other names, characters, places, and incidents are the product
of the author's imagination, and any resemblance to actual events or locales
or persons, living or dead, is entirely coincidental.

ALADDIN PAPERBACKS

An imprint of Simon & Schuster Children's Publishing Division

1230 Avenue of the Americas, New York, NY 10020

Copyright © 2007 by P. W. Catanese

All rights reserved, including the right of reproduction
in whole or in part in any form.

ALADDIN PAPERBACKS and colophon
are trademarks of Simon & Schuster, Inc.

Designed by Karin Paprocki

The text of this book was set in Adobe Jenson.

Manufactured in the United States of America

First Aladdin Paperbacks edition March 2007

2 4 6 8 10 9 7 5 3 1

Library of Congress Control Number 2006930235

ISBN-13: 978-1-4169-1252-1 — ISBN-10: 1-4169-1252-5

✳ ✳ ✳

For everyone who calls me uncle:
Jake, Amy, Emma, Dan, Catie, Allie, and Aaron

✳

The first time the unlucky boy saw the stranger, it was only for an instant. Tom Holly was eating a piece of bread with a smear of honey on top when he spotted a figure on the top of the hill on the other side of the stream. Before he went to the window for a closer look, he put the bread on his plate. When he looked up again, the stranger was gone. Tom frowned, wondering how he'd disappeared so quickly.

The glimpse was fleeting, but Tom thought there was something odd about the fellow he'd seen silhouetted against the orange sky near the setting sun. He tried to recall exactly what the shape looked like. He'd gotten the impression of a small figure—not a boy like himself, but a tiny old man with twiggy arms and legs, and a large head topped by a floppy, wide-brimmed hat. Tom stepped out of the little house where he lived alone. He sat on the stump by the front door and peered at the hill until it was dark. But he didn't see the stranger again that evening.

Tom fell asleep thinking about the oddly shaped man. "Just another curious visitor," he said quietly to himself.

It wasn't unusual for someone to lurk near his home on the island in the stream, trying to get a glimpse of the cursed boy. Sometimes a group of children would come on a dare, seeing who would be brave enough to get closer. They might even throw stones at his shack of a house. Father said they did it because they were afraid. That was an easy problem to fix: Tom would simply walk toward them, and the children would run away, screaming. "Don't think about that," Tom scolded himself as he eased into sleep. "And don't talk out loud to yourself either," he added, "because that means you're going crazy." And then he groaned and punched his own thigh, since he'd said that last part aloud.

The next morning a finger of sunlight poked through the eastern window and prodded him awake. Birds twittered outside. He swiveled his legs off the side of the bed, stretched, and looked out the window.

The stranger was back. Directly across the stream, next to the big willow, staring at him. Tom leaned over the sill, trying to get a better look, and used his hand to shield the morning sun. It was a strange figure, indeed, with a lumpy torso and a long ragged beard. His clothes were gray, his beard was gray—even his skin looked pale and gray. The figure's face was hidden by the shadow of the wide-brimmed hat, but Tom saw a long, narrow, twisted nose poke into the light.

"Looks like a gnome," Tom said.

He opened the door and stepped outside. The gray

man hadn't disappeared this time. "Hello?" he called, wishing his voice hadn't cracked the way it did.

The stranger stared at him, unmoving. A breeze picked up, causing the willow to rock, and the draping branches swung, like a curtain, across the place where the stranger stood. When they settled back, the stranger was gone. It was as if a magician had waved his cloak and caused the gnome to vanish.

"Weird," Tom said quietly. He raked his fingers through his bright red hair and stared at the tree. The woodpile was nearby, and he selected a sturdy sawed-off branch. He walked down the slope toward the stream, swinging the branch through the tall grass, and stopped on the bank across from the big willow. "Who's there?" he called out. "I saw you. There's no point hiding. Come on out." If the stranger was there, he did not reply. The only sound was the hum of insects in the grass. Tom blinked fast and swallowed loudly. What was the little man doing on the other side of that tree?

He heard the clopping of hooves and saw his father, Gilbert Holly, come over the hill beyond the stream, riding a donkey. His father smiled broadly and waved when he saw Tom.

"Dad!" Tom cried. He pointed at the tree. "Do you see him?"

Gilbert Holly cocked his head and stared toward where Tom had pointed. "See who, Son?" he asked when he'd ridden closer.

"The little gray man," Tom said. "Isn't he there, behind the tree?"

Tom's father frowned and dismounted, leaving the donkey to nibble at the tall grass near the bank of the stream. He was a tall, slight man whose big teeth and plump cheeks reminded many people of a rabbit. "This tree here?" he asked. "There's nobody there that I can see."

Tom's jaw sagged. He peered up into the branches. "You don't see him? He must have climbed it!"

His father walked to the tree. He circled it, staring up into the canopy, thick with feathery leaves on drooping branches. "No one's up there, Son. Are you sure . . . ?"

"It was a little old man . . . like a gnome," Tom said.

His father stared with his mouth tugged to one side of his face. He cleared his throat and said, "Tom . . . I know how lonely it must be here. . . ."

"No, no," Tom protested. "I didn't imagine him! I'm not going mad! I *saw* him. And that's the *second* time!"

His father closed his eyes for a moment and took a deep breath. Then he forced a smile. "Come here, Tom. Closer, so we don't have to shout. A little closer won't do any harm."

Tom sighed, came a few steps forward, and sat on the bank of the stream. His father untied the pair of bags that were draped on the donkey's side. "Food in one, and work for you in the other. You sure you don't mind the work?"

"I like the work," Tom said. "It gives me something to

do." He was talking to his father, but his gaze was fixed on the willow. Where could the gnome have gone? There had to be an explanation, but he didn't want to say another word—his father already thought he was losing his mind. *But I'm not.* "I hope."

"What was that, Tom?" his father said.

"Nothing, Dad," Tom replied.

Gilbert stared with his bottom lip pinched between his teeth. "You haven't been talking to yourself, have you, Son?"

"No," Tom said. "Well . . . not too much. I don't think." He punched his thigh, angry that he'd slipped in front of his father. Gilbert was afraid that Tom would lose his wits, living on this solitary island. One particular worry was that Tom would get into the habit of talking to himself aloud. And now Tom had given him another reason for concern, because his father obviously thought he'd imagined that gnome. Tom frowned, knowing he'd just caused his parents some sleepless nights.

Gilbert spread a blanket on the other shore. He dug an apple from one of the sacks and tossed it toward his son. Tom caught the fruit with two hands, rubbed it on his shirt, and bit into the crisp skin. They babbled for hours, just like the shallow band of glittering water that separated them. His father told Tom about how well the shop was doing, the funny things his mother had said, and all the happenings in the bustling, prosperous town of Penwall. It was ordinary stuff, dull in a reassuring kind of way. After a while, Tom stopped glancing at the tree, trying to catch the gnome peeking out from behind the trunk. He imagined himself living with the rest of the people back in the town instead of alone on his tiny island. The daydream ended suddenly when his father said something that made Tom stretch his neck.

"Don't be afraid when I tell you this, Son. But we've been hearing some rumors, and you ought to know."

Tom leaned forward. "About what, Dad?"

Gilbert stood and paced along the bank of the stream. "You know the Marauders we hear about from time to time?"

Tom nodded. Of course, he'd heard of them. Everyone had. They were the brutish raiders who dwelled somewhere beyond the northern borders. The Marauders would stay away for years, assaulting victims in other far-flung lands, and then suddenly would sweep down like locusts across the hills and valleys of Londria. They terrorized and plundered until the king sent a decent army to fight back, and then they quickly retreated beyond the borders of the kingdom. Seven years might pass, or twice that many, but the Marauders always returned.

"Usually they attack farther north, away from the heart of the kingdom," Gilbert said. "But lately people have been passing through with stories. Villages burned and pillaged, much closer than before. So we fear they may push farther south this time." He pulled a fistful of grass from the ground as he talked, then brushed it off his hands. "Listen, I'm sure you're out of harm's way here, Son. And we hear that the king's army is on the chase, so those dogs will probably turn tail as usual. I wouldn't worry too much about it. If there's any news, I'll be sure to let you know. All right?"

"Sure. Thanks, Dad," Tom said. He tried not to let his smile crumble when he saw his father gather up the blanket.

"I'll see you soon, my boy. Don't forget to fetch the sacks when I'm gone."

"I won't," Tom said. When he scratched the inner corner of one eye, his fingertip came away damp.

"I love you, Son," Gilbert said.

"Love you too, Dad," Tom replied.

His father paused with one hand on the donkey's saddle. His mouth twisted. Then he turned and strode quickly toward the stream.

"Dad, don't!" Tom cried.

"I just want to hug you for a second," his father said. "Just once! It won't do any harm."

"You know it can!" Tom shouted. He stepped backward. "Stay away!"

"You're my son!" his father cried back. He stepped onto the nearest stone in the stream. There was no bridge to Tom's island—they didn't want some innocent person to blunder into danger.

"Dad, *no!*"

Tom's father stepped to the next rock and the next, keeping his arms wide for balance. When he was halfway across the stream, a mossy stone rolled under his foot. His arms flapped and spun as he teetered left and right, like a drunken chicken. He plunged his leg into the knee-deep stream, trying to catch his balance, but his foot slipped and he tumbled facedown into the water.

"Dad! Are you all right?" Tom clutched at the air in front of him. He wanted to run to his father, help him up. But that, of course, would only make it worse. *Twenty paces away*, his father had always told him. *Twenty paces to be sure, Tom.* But even that wasn't a safe buffer after a while. Before long, Tom's bad luck would creep outward, like a flooding pond. That was why he had to live by himself, far from anyone.

Gilbert came up, dripping and sputtering. He sat in the stream with his teeth clenched and his eyes squeezed shut, cupping his elbow. "I'm fine," he said through a grimace.

"No, you got hurt!" Tom said. He took another step back, closer to the little house atop the hill.

"It wasn't your fault," his father said. He winced and sucked air between his teeth as he tried to straighten the arm. "I was just . . ."

"Unlucky," Tom moaned.

"No!" his father shouted, slapping the water with his

8

good hand. He stood cautiously, his clothes still dripping. "I should have known better. It was my fault, not yours."

Tom stared at the ground. "How can you stand it? Having a son who's—"

"That's enough of that! Your mum and I don't regret a thing, Tom. Not a moment since we found you. And we haven't given up trying to . . . *fix* this. Do you understand that, Tom? Look at me, and promise you understand."

There was only one room in the little house that Tom's father had built for him a few years before. It had a stove in the middle, a tiny table with a single chair against one wall, and his bed in a corner.

Tom was in bed but not yet asleep. A bright moon sailed high over the roof, and its thin light washed through the open window at his shoulder. On the table, he could make out the dozens of game pieces, freshly painted. His father carved the items, Tom colored them, and they were sold in his parents' shop in the town of Penwall.

A few hours before, when Tom emptied the sack to see what work his father had brought, he smiled when he saw the carved figures among them: pawns, rooks, bishops, knights, queens, and kings. He didn't exactly know how chess was played, but he understood that each piece had its own peculiar ability and its own role to play in the grand scheme of the game. Something about the chessmen had a magnetic appeal to him, a powerful connection he never quite understood.

There was something else in the sack: a piece of

parchment, folded into a square and sealed with wax. Tom thought he knew what was inside. When he broke the seal and opened the parchment, he saw that he was right.

It was stuffed with four-leaf clovers, dozens of them, fading from living green to deathly brown. His mother must have plucked them herself. Tom pictured her scouring the meadow on her hands and knees. How many hours had she spent gathering these useless weeds? At least the clover didn't cost anything; that wasn't always the case with the gifts his parents sent. There was a small chest at the foot of Tom's bed, filled with stuff that wasn't at all free. He had tokens made of iron and silver. Horseshoes. Tiny bits of rolled cloth, covered with strange words or symbols or numbers. At least twenty rabbits' feet. Amulets in the shape of eyes, frogs, crescent moons, horns, scorpions, and ladybirds. Rings of every color and metal. Strings of beads. Little sacks of ash leaves and foul-smelling herbs. Medallions inscribed with magic squares of letters and numbers. Pieces of amber. The dried paw of a monkey. Tom sighed heavily, thinking of that stash. He knew his parents had paid a steep price for some of those supposedly magical things, but none of them worked. Not even one. Not even once.

Tom refolded the parchment with the clovers inside, and set it on the windowsill beside his bed. He stretched his arms and closed his eyes, and began to think about the great questions of his life as he often did before drifting off to sleep. There was his curse—where did it come from? Did somebody hex him long ago, some witch or warlock? And why? Who would do such a thing to a helpless child?

He wondered, too, about where he'd come from. His mother and father, Joan and Gilbert Holly, had found him when he was just a baby, in a time that Tom could not remember. They'd given him all the love he could want, and more than most would give to a cursed child that wasn't even theirs. They were so good to him that it made Tom feel guilty when he wondered who his real parents were and where they were now. "Somewhere out there," he whispered. The thought made him open his eyes to gaze into the moonlit night.

Filling the window, just an arm's length away, was the dimly lit face of the gnome.

A jolt ran from Tom's toes to the top of his head, and he thrashed under the covers. A scream was launched from his lungs, snagged momentarily in the back of his throat, and then burst out in a high squeal.

"Shet yer face," the stranger snarled.

"Buh . . . buh . . ." Tom sputtered.

"'Buh'! 'Buh'!" the gnome cried, mocking him. He walked away from the window, out of sight. Tom pulled the blanket to his mouth and chewed on the edge.

"Well?" shouted the gruff voice, right into his ear.

Tom screamed again, even louder. The stranger was standing beside his bed, though Tom hadn't heard the door open. *How did he get in so fast?* Tom scrabbled backward, pushing with his arms and legs until his shoulders met the wall. His heart pounded like a blacksmith's hammer as he stared at the tiny silhouette of the gnome.

"You . . . you . . ." Tom tried to say, but the air was gone from his lungs.

"Me? *Me?*" the gnome shrieked. It was too dark to see his face, but Tom saw him put his hands on his waist and tilt his head to one side.

Tom gulped and stuttered out some words. "Y-you can't be here! It isn't s-s-safe!"

The little gray man leaned closer. "What do ye mean, 'isn't s-s-safe'?"

Tom sat up in bed, keeping his back pressed to the wall. He breathed through his mouth, trying to control the violent heaving of his chest. "I'm c-cursed. I bring bad luck to anyone who comes near me. And you're *way too close right now!*"

The stranger stuck out his tongue and waved at the air. The hand was far too big for the tiny body to which it was attached. And, even odder, the gnome had sticks bound to the length of his arms, held in place by fine straps of leather or bark, as if splints were needed to hold his arms together. The strange man couldn't have been more than three feet tall. He wore a filthy coat over a filthy shirt and filthy leggings, and his enormous feet were shod with filthy boots.

"Bah," the gnome said. "Yer curse won't touch me, ye little idjit."

"Wh-why not?"

"Because I SAID IT WON'T!" the gnome bellowed, taking a great leap into the air. His knees reached up to his ears, and in his fury he grabbed his beard with both hands and pulled it wide to either side of his face.

"All right, all right!" Tom shouted back. He was afraid the little man might break himself into pieces. The gnome grunted and paced back and forth across the dark room, muttering all the while. Tom eased his way across the bed and onto the floor, trying not to make a sound. He reached toward the night table beside his bed.

The gnome whirled and shouted again, "WHAT DO YE THINK YE'RE DOING?!"

"I just want to light a candle," Tom said. "I can't see a thing."

The gnome went back to muttering and pacing. Tom shook his head and grabbed the candle that he'd snuffed out earlier. He carried it to the stove and opened its door. There were embers left from when he'd cooked his porridge. He blew on them, and they glowed orange, hot enough to ignite the wick when he pressed it against them. With the candle in hand, he went to his kitchen table and sat, staring at the odd little intruder who still stomped furiously around the room.

"What—," Tom started to say aloud, before remembering that some things were better said inwardly. *What a face*, he thought. It was gnarled and lined like a mountaintop tree, with a twisted nose as long and narrow as a finger, and a snarled, grimy beard that hung to the knees. The skin was wrinkled and parched, without a hint of pink or tan to the ashen pallor. The gnome's gray hair looked like it had never been cut in all his years. It flowed out from under his broad, floppy hat and spilled across his shoulders. His enormous ears were tattered at the edges like dried autumn leaves, and there was a thicket of white hairs sprouting from the ear holes.

The strange man finally came to a stop, with his back to Tom. He pulled off the hat, revealing a thin nest of tangled hair, and smacked himself three times on the forehead with the heel of one hand. "Urg!" he cried. "Urg! URG!"

"What's the matter with you?" Tom ventured. He cringed as the gnome whirled upon him again.

"What's the matter with *me?*" The gnome's eyes bulged, and he gnashed his teeth. "I'm not the one who's cursed, am I?" When Tom didn't answer in a flash, he screamed it louder. "AM I!"

"No." Tom edged backward, keeping the table between him and the stranger. He took a deep breath, wondering if he dared to say another word. But there was something he had to know. His voice came out in a squeak. "Why are you here?"

The gnome narrowed his eyes and stared, with his

mustache twitching on one side. He came to the other side of the table and leaned on it. "I have a deed that needs doing. And ye're going to do it for me."

Tom stared back, blinking fast. "Me? Why do you need me?"

The gnome clasped his hands and rubbed them, making a raspy sound. His gaze sparkled. "Because yer . . . *affliction* will come in handy."

Tom shifted his weight uneasily from one foot to the other. "I don't understand. . . . And besides . . ." He wanted to ask, *Who would do anything for a nut like you?* But he simply said, "Why should I help you?"

The gnome's temper exploded again. His face puckered in the middle until it seemed like it might collapse on itself. He pulled the brim of his hat down on both sides of his head. At last he took a deep breath and regained his composure. He even tried to smile—a gesture that, given the broken, darkened condition of his teeth, was even more troubling than his grimace. "Because, little *boy*"—he said "boy" as if it were a species of vermin—"I can end this curse of yers."

Tom gasped aloud. His heart threw itself against his ribs, like a bird battering the bars of its cage. "You can? But . . . I don't even know how I got this curse, or why. What do you know about it? How can you end it?"

The gnome grinned smugly and folded his arms, creasing his tangled beard. "Ye'll have to trust me."

It occurred to Tom that this stranger was, at first

impression, anyway, the least trustworthy soul he'd ever encountered. But his head felt light at even the suggestion that his curse could be lifted. "Well," he said, "I'd like to get rid of it, of course . . . but what would you need me to do?"

"THAT'S NONE OF YER BUSINESS!" the gnome shouted, shaking a fist.

Tom gave his head a shake, as if that could help him unscramble the gnome's nonsense. "Of *course* it's my business. I can't do something for you if you don't tell me what it is!"

The gnome snorted. "What a stupid lump of snot ye are. That's enough questions! All ye need to know is we're going on a journey, ye and me. And ye're going to do exactly as I say. And if ye can accomplish the deed I need done, I'll end this hex of yers. Is that clear enough? Eh?"

"But how—"

"SHET YER FACE, YE IDJIT!" the gnome roared, leaping up and down. "NO MORE STUPID QUESTIONS! IT'S NO OR NOW! NEVER OR YES! WHAT WILL IT BE?"

3

Tom was in bed again with his hands clutching the hair behind his ears. He talked aloud and answered his own questions.

"How could you say no? What if the gnome could have cured me?

"But that little fellow was crazy. . . . Who knows if he was telling the truth? He was probably up to no good! I was afraid to go with him.

"It was worth the risk! What am I supposed to do—live the rest of my life alone in this house?

"There must be another way . . .

"There *is* no other way—that gnome may have been the only chance, and now he's gone!"

Tom wailed and kicked the blankets onto the floor. "I really will go crazy here," he cried. He pounded the wall with a fist and lurched upright, pressing his palms into eyes that were suddenly hot with tears. When he took his hands away from his face, he saw a strange glow through one of the windows.

"Too early for sunrise," he said, sniffing and wiping his nose with his sleeve. He stood and walked to the window, gulping past a lump that suddenly formed in his throat. The glow was on the horizon, orange and flickering. And it came from the direction of the town where his mother and father lived.

Tom ran the first mile, and then walked until he thought he could run again. He ran and walked and ran and walked some more, and each time the distance he could run shrank until he could run no longer.

The footpath from his home on the stream brought him to the main road to Penwall. The wind blew his way, and Tom's heart twisted as he caught a whiff of burning wood. The sky blushed with the rising of the sun, and he saw thick, black smoke snaking to the heavens.

Penwall was ablaze.

Tom crossed the arching stone bridge at the edge of the town on weak, rubbery legs. His jaw sagged and his hands trembled. He hadn't been able to visit this place for many years, but he remembered what it looked like. There was once a happy, busy street lined with shops. When you walked its length, the bakers, tailors, cobblers, confectioners, candle makers, jewelers, and all the others would step outside and stand, smiling by their wares, keen to sell. Among them, of course, would be his parents.

It was gone now, all of it. Every building had been put to flame, even the smaller ones on the side roads. Most of the burning was complete, with only blackened timbers remaining, but flames still roared up here and there as the voracious fire gnawed on scraps of wood. The buildings shuddered and groaned and popped and hissed in various stages of slow collapse. The heat of the inferno warped the air, and flakes of ash fluttered down like snow.

Not far down the road, Tom saw his parents' shop, now just a smoky ruin. He clasped his hands on top of his head and stared.

"Mum? Dad?" He didn't hear an answer. Nor did he see anyone. Not a soul.

"Where is everyone?" he finally shouted.

"They ran," said a weak voice from behind him. Tom turned and saw a woman, ancient and feeble, coming out from hiding under the stone bridge. She struggled up the steep bank and hobbled toward him, leaning heavily on a walking stick. "But I couldn't run. So I hid. And I *saw*."

Tom stepped back, keeping his distance. Not only because of his bad luck, but because of the haunted, lost look in the woman's red-rimmed eyes.

"Was it the Marauders?" he asked her.

"Of course," the woman said, still limping toward him. "But not just them. Something else, too." She stopped for a moment to control the shuddering that overtook her body. She leaned on the staff with her head bowed and her white hair dangling in front of her face, waiting for the shaking to pass.

"Something else?" Tom asked. "What?"

The old woman's head snapped up. Her eyes bulged, and she looked around like a frightened mouse. "A *monster*," she said hoarsely. "A monster came first. Frightened everyone away. Its face was so horrible, nobody could stand to look. The strongest men quailed before it and ran away, weeping."

"Everyone ran? They didn't all die?" Tom felt a feathery touch of hope.

"Most ran, except the few that hid in their homes or tried to fight. The Marauders came and dealt with those poor souls. Then they stole everything they could, and set fire to all the buildings. And went on to the next town, I suppose."

Tom was so busy hoping that his parents had run away and wondering how he might find them, he didn't notice the old woman creeping toward him as she spoke. She was nearly close enough to touch him now, and she reached out with a twisted, clutching hand.

"But you'll help me, won't you? There's a nice boy. See if there's anything left in some of those shops ... a penny or two, a scrap of food. Those villains must've left something behind, eh?"

"No—get away! Don't touch me!" Tom said, hopping back.

Her mouth curled up in a smile that failed to reassure. "Stay, little friend, and help me!" She took another step, but her walking stick suddenly snapped in the middle.

The old woman toppled like a tree and hit the ground where ash billowed in every direction.

"No," she moaned as Tom took another step back. She raised a twisted hand and clawed at the air. "Come help me up! I can't do it myself!"

Tom bit his lip. His voice shook when he replied. "I can't—something worse will happen. You don't want my help," Tom said.

"Come back here!" she called out. "I'm not going to hurt you! Where are you going? Have mercy on an old woman!"

"I'm sorry, I can't!" Tom turned and ran down the street between the cremated rows of shops. Her pleas faded away, lost among the sizzle and crackle of the embers, and Tom's eyes stung from smoke and tears.

CHAPTER

4

On the far side of town, away from the woman he didn't dare assist, Tom leaned on a fence post by the side of the road. He pulled up the collar of his shirt and wiped his eyes, then covered his face with his hands. "I couldn't even help her stand up," he whispered.

"Bah. She'll get up eventually," said an unpleasant voice beside him, instantly recognizable.

Tom's head shot up from his hands. For an instant he was glad to see a familiar face, even if it belonged to such an obnoxious character. But the gladness evaporated when he saw the gnome's grin and heard his chuckle.

"How can you laugh?" Tom cried. "Look what the Marauders did!"

The gnome looked back at the town, raising his eyebrows. "Quite the mischief makers. Naughty, naughty!" He rubbed one gnarly index finger across the other.

Tom's glare lingered. "How do you do that, anyway? Sneak up without me seeing you? And you disappear, too."

The gnome's satisfied expression darkened. "Questions, questions. Stick yer nose where it don't belong and it may get bitten off, idjit."

Tom's hands clenched into rock-hard fists. He'd never put a hand in anger on anyone. But he dearly wanted to punch this miserable little man, right in his swollen belly. "Do you know where everyone went? The people who lived here?"

The gnome stuck his lower lip out and scanned the horizon. "Bolted wike widdle fwightened wabbits, of course. I suppose ye're wondering where yer darling mummy and daddy went to. What's the matter—did the Marauders get them? Or did they run away and leave ye behind? It's one or the other, ain't it? Boo hoo, does that make ye sad?" The gnome put his fists beside his eyes and twisted them, pretending to cry. "Maybe they decided to leave their little curse behind for good."

"No," Tom said. His legs trembled. "They wouldn't do that. They'll come back for me."

The gnome laughed. "If ye say so, little fool!" He doffed his hat, punched the inside of it to make the point stand tall, and put it back on his sparsely haired head. "Have a lovely day," he said, and walked away.

Tom rubbed his hands across his face and let out a deep breath. "Wait!" he cried.

The gnome stopped with his back to Tom, and slowly turned his head. His neck was strangely elastic—his shoulders barely moved yet the head swiveled almost entirely around. One of the gnome's eyes was nearly closed and the other glittered brightly, expectantly. "What do ye want now?"

"I want . . ." Tom closed his eyes for a moment and cleared his throat. *Just say it.* His voice was hoarse from the smoke he'd inhaled. "I want to end my curse. I'll do this thing for you."

The gnome turned completely around, untwisting his neck. "What, ye're not going to run crying, looking for yer mummy and daddy?"

Tom pressed his lips together and looked back at the smoldering wreck that used to be Penwall. More than anything, he wanted to look for his parents. But he couldn't. Not yet. If he went to find them, he'd only bring them more bad luck. Besides, he was starting to wonder if this, the burning of Penwall, was because of him. *What if it stuck to Dad and followed him home?*

He turned back to the gnome. "How long will it take, this thing you want me to do?"

"As long as it takes, that's how long it will take." The gnome snarled. "Will ye do it?"

Tom nodded. The gnome's mouth curled into a crafty grin. He came toward Tom on oversized feet, taking long, slow steps as if moving underwater. "Ye'll do exactly as I say?"

"Yes."

"And ye won't ask questions?"

Tom tilted his head to one side. "I'll probably ask them. You don't have to answer them."

The gnome stopped, one stride away, and folded his arms. "Then I guess we have a deal."

"But you'll cure me," Tom said quietly. He was afraid to say it too loud, as if that might frighten the notion away. "You can really do that?"

"There ye go with yer *questions*," the gnome said sourly, spitting out the last word like a bug that had flown into his mouth.

Tom put his hand out. "I do this thing for you, and you end the curse. That's the bargain. I want to shake on it."

The gnome glared at Tom's hand, and his face flushed a dark, bruised shade of purple. "And that's another condition—don't ye *ever* touch me! NEVER!" He clenched his teeth, seized his beard with both hands, and tugged it so hard to the right that Tom thought the whole thing might come out by the roots.

"All right, all right!" Tom said. "I'll just take your word for it."

The gnome stared at Tom with narrowed eyes and waited until his chest stopped heaving before he spoke again. "Oh ye will, will ye? Then it's time to begin." He pointed a long, crooked finger at the road that led north, away from Penwall. "That way."

Tom stared at the road. "Now?"

"Yes, now!" snapped the gnome. "What, do ye have something else to do?"

"But I don't have any food or water. . . ."

"JEST DO EXACTLY AS I SAY!" the gnome bellowed, springing high into the air and flailing his arms. "THAT'S THE BARGAIN!"

"Right, right!" Tom said. "Yeesh!" He'd seen the gnome lose his temper many times now, and noticed something odd. When the little man worked himself into a rage, another look came into his eye: a kind of rapture. It was as if the only thing that made him truly happy was to be utterly filled with anger and bile.

There was no reasoning with the gnome, so Tom started to walk. As far as he knew, this road led to a wilder part of the country. "Where am I—" The question died in his mouth when he turned around and saw that the gnome was no longer there.

CHAPTER

5

"Here's the trouble, Tom," he said to himself as he walked. "What if Dad was right, and you're going batty from living by yourself and you're just imagining this gnome?"

It was an unsettling thought. He turned and looked back toward Penwall. He'd come so far that he could no longer see the thin stream of smoke rising from the charred, abandoned town. His heart fluttered as he thought about his mother and father, and the dreadful possibility that he might never see them again.

"Am I even doing the right thing?" he asked the distance. But the only answer was the grumbling of his hungry belly. Next to the road, he found grapevines clutching the trees and wild berries farther along the way. "Lucky me," he said, with juice running down his chin.

The kingdom of Londria was a green, green place. It was made of hills, valleys, dales, meadows, and forests, with so many folds and buckles in the land that a person could rarely see more than a mile ahead of where he stood. One never walked on the horizontal in Londria;

the way always rose or fell. Nor could one wander far without crossing a bridge because it was also a watery place, threaded by numerous rivers and streams that trickled and gushed and filled a thousand rippling lakes and peaceful ponds. The chatter of crickets and twitter of birds filled the sky. Willows were more abundant than any other tree by far, rocking like drowsy soft-shouldered giants with their wide, green sleeves billowing in the breezes.

In the shade of one of those willows, next to one of those streams, Tom went to wash his sticky, juice-stained hands. He slid down the steep bank, and heard the croaks and plunks of frightened frogs leaping into the water.

When he clambered up the bank again, he noticed someone coming his way from the road ahead. It was a cart pulled by a single horse, with only the driver aboard. The cart was about to cross the narrow wooden bridge that spanned the stream. "I'd better get out of the way," Tom said quietly. He learned long ago that it was easier to avoid strangers than it was to explain why they shouldn't come near him. So he stepped off the path and hid himself in the woods.

When the man had driven his cart halfway across the bridge, he was attacked.

Two robbers burst out of the forest and blocked the cart's path. The shorter one aimed a bow and arrow at the driver. The other, a tall, gangly, crude-looking sort, wielded a long, heavy club. Behind the cart, another robber sprang up from under the bridge and mounted the cart from the rear. The driver tried to spur his horse and ride past the robbers before him, but the third robber seized him from behind and threw him off the cart.

Tom felt a fire light up inside him as he witnessed the robbery. His chest heaved and his breath whistled keenly out of his nose as he saw the poor driver rise to his feet, only to be driven down again by a fierce whack from the tall robber's club. The driver covered his head and cowered on the ground as the robbers stole everything the man had—a single sack of goods from the cart and a pouch that hung from his belt. They untied his horse and led it away, laughing at the poor man who still lay on the planks of the bridge. The horse and the robbers disappeared down a dark path in the forest by the side of the road.

Tom came out of hiding and jogged toward the man, wondering if he was all right. He stopped twenty paces away, just as the man lifted his head. One of his eyes was swollen shut, and blood trickled from his nose.

The man spotted Tom. "They took it all!" he cried. "Every bit!"

"I saw what happened," Tom said. "I'm so sorry."

"Even my poor horse. What'll I do now? How will I eat? How will I work? Curse them! Curse those robbers!" The man hammered the planks with his fist.

Curse them. The words echoed in Tom's head. He

looked at the man's face and saw the eyes, runny and red-rimmed, the skin flushed and slick with sweat, the mouth twisted with anguish. Tom thought about Penwall in flames, his parents who were homeless or worse, and the poor old woman he couldn't help to her feet. All the despair that had pooled up inside him ignited, like oil in a shattered lamp. *Curse those robbers.* "Good idea!" he said, clenching his teeth and lowering his head. He stomped the ground with one foot and strode toward the forest's path.

"What—where are you going, boy?" the man cried. "Don't go in there—those men are dangerous! They'll hurt you!"

"I'm dangerous too," Tom called over his shoulder as he plunged into the shadows of the trees. "Wait for me there."

It didn't take long to catch up to the robbers. The path led to a clearing in the forest, where they had their camp. The horse was tethered to a tree, and the scoundrels were already picking through the stolen goods. Tom watched from his hiding place as the shorter one turned the pouch upside down, spilling coins into his waiting palm. The tallest and nastiest one upended the stolen sack.

Wait, Tom thought. *There were three. Where's the third one?* The answer came when a voice rang out behind him.

"You're a nosy little runt, aren't you?"

Tom turned and saw the third robber, a powerful-looking, black-bearded man, reaching down to grab him by the front of his shirt. He let himself fall, avoiding the robber's grasp, and used his arms and legs to walk himself backward on the ground.

The black-bearded robber chuckled. "Looky here, Toothless," he said. "This boy thinks he's the sheriff. Or maybe he came to steal what we just rightfully robbed."

Tom glanced over his shoulder at the tallest robber, the one called Toothless. The ugly fellow had been hunched over the stolen goods, but he stood up to his full, towering height, and bared an ugly smile that was indeed nearly toothless—just a handful of blackened, rotten teeth populated his gums. Something terrible had happened to his face once; the nose was flat and broken, and the skin was scratched and scarred. "Stupid boy," he said, although his words were slurred and hard to understand due to the terrible state of his mouth. There was an ax in a stump nearby. The blade squealed as Toothless pried it from the wood.

Tom felt his foot being pinned to the ground by a boot, and he couldn't crawl backward anymore. He looked up at the black-bearded robber, who pulled a knife from his belt and stared down with a cruel grin. "Something should have happened by now," Tom said.

"Oh really? Like what?" said the black-bearded man, sneering down at him.

Tom felt a queer sensation inside his head. It felt this

way sometimes, just before bad luck would strike. It was like a feather tickling the inside of his skull, or a tiny ant crawling over the folds of his brain. He heard the crack of old, dry wood from high overhead. Tom looked up and saw a thick, dead branch plummeting from the upper reaches of the tree he was under. The dark shape slowly turned in the air, making not another sound until it struck the black-bearded robber on the top of his head. The robber's eyelids fluttered, and he fell face-first onto the ground, as heavy and senseless as a sack of dirt.

The one called Toothless slapped his knee and doubled over, laughing merrily. "Ha! Did ya see that, Squint? Looks like we only got to split it two ways now!" The one called Squint shrugged and began to sort the stolen coins into two piles instead of three.

Tom stood up and pointed a finger at the loot. "Leave that stuff where it is and get out of here. Unless you want something bad to happen to you, too. And it will!"

Toothless laughed even harder, and Squint looked at Tom with narrowed eyes. "Are you insane, little boy? That fellow there is Toothless John, the nastiest rogue you'll ever meet. If I were you, I'd run away before he gathers his wits. Trust me, he doesn't like little boys."

"Too late," muttered Toothless John, mopping at his eyes with the skin of his wrist. He brought the ax up, whipped it back over his shoulder, and snapped his arm down again to hurl it in Tom's direction.

Tom threw his hands up in front of his face. But,

through the gaps between his fingers, he saw the handle of the ax fly harmlessly by. The head of the ax had slipped off the handle when Toothless coiled it behind his shoulder, and flown the opposite way. It whistled through the air and its blunt side struck Squint in the forehead. Squint's eyes rolled up, flashing white, and his tongue lolled. He tottered and fell, planting the back of his head into the forest floor.

Toothless stared stupidly at Squint, and then at the black-bearded man. His chin bobbed up and down.

"I told you something bad would happen," Tom said.

"Y-you *m-made* that happen?" sputtered Toothless.

Tom nodded. "Last chance," he said, stepping forward. He lowered his brow and raised his hands, with the fingers curled like the claws of a cat. "Run away, or you're next."

Toothless yelped, and he turned and ran without considering what lay in his path, which happened to be a tree that didn't yield an inch when he drove his face into it. He staggered back with his hands covering his nose, which was broken anew. His heel caught on a stone and he fell onto the fire. He leaped up, slapped his rear to put out the flames, and ran squealing into the woods, trailing smoke from his hindquarters.

Tom looked at the other robbers, lying still on the ground. He saw the black-bearded fellow's chest move up and down, and the other one's foot twitching. "That's good," he said. He didn't want to hurt anyone too badly, no matter how much they deserved it. His stomach was already in knots, thinking about how much pain he'd caused. He scooped up the stolen goods, stuffed them back into the sack, and untied the horse.

A fowl had been roasting on the fire, but had fallen onto the ground when Toothless stumbled into the flames. "No sense wasting that," Tom said. *Hey, stop saying things out loud,* he scolded himself. *You sound like a lunatic!* He picked up the roasted bird, wiped off the dirt and bits of leaf, and tore away a drumstick to gnaw on as he led the horse out of the woods.

"Hoo, hoo!" came the voice of the gnome from above, startling him. The little gray man was sitting on the branch of a tree, grinning broadly and swinging his skinny legs. "That was entertaining! Dishing out the punishment now, aren't we? Silly boy, it never occurred to ye that yer curse might be useful, did it?"

Tom stopped to look up at the gnome, and the horse nuzzled his ear. "No," he said. "I never did anything like that before. Why would I?"

"Because it's *fun*, for one thing! Ha! Well, ye've earned a pretty penny today. And got yerself some transportation, too! Clever, clever!"

Tom pursed his lips and frowned up at the gnome. "What do you mean? I'm giving this back to the man they robbed."

The gnome's eyes goggled, and his legs froze in midswing. "What? WHAT? Are ye dense? Didn't yer parents teach ye good sense? Jest take the loot!"

"They did teach me good sense. And manners, too," Tom said. "This stuff isn't mine."

"WHO CARES?" screeched the gnome. "DO YE HAVE DUNG FOR BRAINS? WHO THE DEVIL CARES?"

"Me," Tom said. "And him," he added, jutting his chin toward the end of the path, where he hoped the robbers' victim was still waiting.

As Tom led the horse out of the forest, he heard the gnome muttering behind him. "What sort of dunderhead am I working with here? I've stepped in cow turds smarter than him. . . ."

When Tom came out of the woods, the man's face rose up from his cupped hands. The fellow's eyes widened when he saw the horse and the pack slung over Tom's shoulder. The smile that blossomed on his face warmed Tom's heart.

The man began to race toward him. "Stop!" cried Tom, holding up a palm, and the man did, with a puzzled expression. Tom laid the sack on the ground beside the horse and backed away. "Please . . . don't come any closer. It's all there," he said. "And some roasted fowl too, if you're hungry."

"I don't know what to say," the fellow said, shaking his head. "How did you . . . ?"

"I just got lucky," Tom replied. Something occurred to him. "You weren't on your way to Penwall, were you?"

"I was," said the man.

"It's gone," Tom said.

The smile disappeared from the man's face. "The Marauders?"

Tom nodded.

The fellow's shoulders sagged. "I'm from Rookington. They burned that too, you know." He held out his hand. "Still, I'd like to shake your hand, young man. I don't know how you got my things back, but it was brave of you to even try."

"No . . . it's better if you don't come closer," Tom said.

The man smiled. "What a curious boy you are. Take this, at least." He dug into his sack of coins and tossed three gold pieces to Tom.

"Thank you, sir," Tom said, pocketing them. "Thank you very much."

"You deserve it. Best of luck to you," said the man. He carried his sack to the cart that was still on the bridge.

As Tom watched the man toss his belongings into the cart, he felt that uneasy sensation inside his head. "Oh no," Tom said, and the man looked at him to see what the trouble might be. There was a groaning sound, and a snap, and the old bridge across the stream sagged on one side. The cart tipped sideways, balanced on two wheels for a moment, and then tumbled into the stream as the poor man leaped to safety. The horse, frightened by the noise, reared up and dashed away, hurtling down the road. The fellow looked at the smashed cart and the vanishing horse, turned his face to the sky, and wailed. Then he saw his bag of goods floating down the stream, and stumbled down the bank to wade after it.

Tom sighed, hung down his head, and went on with his journey.

6

A while later, just as Tom was beginning to wonder if he was still heading the right way, he saw the gnome waiting by the side of the road with his arms folded and the tip of one boot tapping the ground. Tom turned away, refusing to look, when he saw the smirk on the gnome's face.

"Serves ye right," the gnome said.

"You mean what happened at the bridge? I got too close, that's all. I was trying to help."

"Help! Ha! Help yerself, that's my motto."

"It isn't mine," Tom grumbled. "My dad always says we were born to help one another." He finished gnawing the meat off the drumstick, and tossed the bone into the brush by the side of the path.

"Oh, is that what he says? Well, I guess the idjit nut didn't fall far from the idjit tree." The gnome peered up at Tom as he walked beside him. "Say, what's the matter with yer face?"

Tom put his hand to his cheek, wondering if he was bleeding. "What do you mean?"

"It's covered with spots."

"Spots . . . You mean my freckles?"

"If that's what ye call those ugly things."

Tom scowled. "Lots of people have freckles. Especially people with red hair. My mum says they're beautiful."

The gnome shrugged. "Then she's stupid too. Or a liar."

Tom felt his lips twitch and his nostrils flare. "You know what? You're a nasty little man. I'm getting tired of you."

The gnome threw up his enormous hands. "I'm jest being honest!"

Tom looked up to the skies and shook his head. "What's your name, anyway?" he asked a while later.

"None of yer blooming business, that's my blooming name," the gnome grumbled.

"What? You're afraid to tell me your name?"

The gnome turned to face Tom. "*Afraid?* Me, afraid? Ye don't know what *afraid* is, boy. But ye will, when we get where we're going."

All the moisture left Tom's mouth. "Where's that?"

A sly smile crept onto the gnome's gnarled face. "The Dark Dell."

Tom coughed. "We're going to the Dark Dell? But . . . *nobody's* supposed to go to the Dark Dell."

"Ye've heard of it, eh?"

Yeah, I've heard of it, Tom thought. *And there's a reason it's called the Dark Dell. Because something terrible is supposed to live there. A creature so horrible, it can drive a man crazy if he only looks at it.* "Nobody in their right mind goes to the Dark Dell," he said.

"'Tis a lovely place." The gnome sighed. "But first we have one stop along the way."

"Where—"

"AGH! AGAIN THE QUESTIONS! SHET YER MOUTH!!"

Near the end of the day they left the road and walked up a hill that was studded with steep, craggy ledges. There was no path, but the gnome pointed the way.

"Through there," said the gnome, jabbing his thumb toward a vertical crack in a tall ledge. It was just wide enough for Tom to scrape his way through. Overhead, fallen stones had sealed off the top of the passage, creating a crude tunnel that twisted left and right. "It's getting dark," Tom said.

"Never ye mind," the voice grumbled from behind.

The passage opened into a larger chamber; how big, Tom could not tell. "What are we doing here? Is this the Dark Dell?"

"'Is this the Dark Dell?'" mimicked the gnome. "Idjit, jest because it's dark doesn't make it the Dark Dell! Do ye not know the difference between a hole in the ground and a dell? Now, if ye'll stop saying stupid things for a minute and look around, ye might find something useful."

Tom took advantage of the darkness to stick his tongue

out in the direction of the gnome. Then he looked about him. He saw something odd: a dim yellow glow at the level of his feet, in one corner of the chamber.

"What is that?" he whispered.

"Go see, foolish boy," hissed the gnome.

Tom dropped to his hands and knees, and crawled toward the glow. There was a crack in the stone ledge that formed that end of the chamber. When he peered inside, he saw an enormous fat toad, glowing softly.

"What are ye waiting for? Pick it up!" the gnome grumbled.

Tom reached in with two hands and gently slid them under the soft, warty bulk of the toad. He pulled it out gently, grimacing, knowing that toads often left a nasty present in your hand when you tried to pick them up. But this paunchy specimen didn't struggle at all or befoul him. It nestled comfortably, so bulky that it overflowed Tom's palms on both sides. The creature even lifted its wide head to look at him with bulging, watery eyes.

"What is this thing?" he asked.

"A glow-toad, stupid. What else would ye call it?"

Tom smiled down at the gleaming toad and used a thumb to stroke its chin. When he did, the creature's glow abruptly brightened, flooding the room with pale yellow light.

Now that there was enough light to see, Tom looked around the chamber, and his smile eroded. In this damp, lightless hole in the earth, someone had made a home. The simple furnishings reminded Tom of his own forsaken house on the island in the stream. There was a bed, a table and a chair . . . all tiny, old, and worn. His nose wrinkled at the smell of mold and decay. "Is this . . . where you live?" Tom asked.

"Will yer fool questions never end?" muttered the gnome, pushing his knuckles into his ears. "Jest open up that chest over there, ye meddlesome rat."

Tom turned and saw a wooden chest behind him. He cradled the glow-toad in the crook of his arm and lifted the lid. The hinges were made of rotten leather that tore as easily as wet parchment, so the lid broke away and clattered to the ground when he raised it. A thick plume of dust shot into the air.

"Careful, muttonhead!"

"Sorry," Tom said, coughing. The sour taste of dust filled his mouth as he looked inside the open chest. There was a mishmash of items inside. Pots and pans, and empty jars with round corks. A child's doll. An old pair of boots, worn through at the toes, made for a long, thin pair of feet. Tom reached in and tugged on something made of heavy cloth. He lifted out a wide-brimmed, pointed hat, much like the one the gnome wore. A moth took flight from one of its folds and flittered toward the glow of the toad. The glow-toad waited until it was near, and then lunged, thrusting out its fat, sticky tongue. It gobbled the bug down with bits of wing crumbling out of the corners of its mouth.

Tom looked at the gnome. "This is your home, isn't it?"

"Never mind that. See that big jar? Put the glow-toad inside. And there's a pack in that chest that ye can take, to hold the jar. Stuff an extra sack in there too. Take the tinderbox. And anything else ye think ye might need."

Tom looked around the sad little place, and back into the glaring eyes of the gnome.

"You *do* live here," Tom said. He glanced at the doll in the chest. It was made of wood, with jointed arms and legs, and missing one hand and one foot. "And you're just as lonely as me. Aren't you?"

The gnome squeezed words out between lips pressed tight together. "It's the Dark Dell tomorrow, nosy pig. So don't fritter away what may be yer last night on stupid questions. Go to sleep. I'll see yer ugly face in the morning." And the gnome stomped out of the chamber, whispering further insults that Tom could barely hear.

Tom stepped out of the crack in the ledge into the ruddy light of dawn. The gnome was there, crouched atop a boulder like a vulture. His customary sneer was already engraved on his ashen face.

"I'm hungry," Tom said, knowing that "good morning" would be a waste of breath.

"Whiny brat. There are some glumberries back there," the gnome said, jabbing a thumb over his shoulder. "Fill your little sack with them."

Tom followed the gesture and found a thorny bush covered with hundreds of berries. It was a kind he'd never seen before: plump, oval, and dark red—nearly black—in color. "Glumberries," he said, remembering the name. He plucked one off the bush and popped it into his mouth. A moment later he was spitting violently, wiping his tongue with the cuff of his sleeve, and willing himself not to vomit.

"*Aaagh!*" he cried. "*Blech!* What was that? You can't eat those!"

"I never told ye to eat them," said the gnome, chuckling. "I jest told ye to fill yer sack. When are ye going to start to listen, ye boneheaded brat?"

* * *

"Are we getting close?" Tom asked.

"Jest around this bend," the gnome grumbled. He added something else under his breath, but all Tom could hear was the word "question," and another word his father told him he should never say.

The path had gotten wilder, narrowing to a thin trace of sparsely covered ground that pierced a weedy meadow. Tom was surprised there was a trail at all, so near a place with such a frightening reputation. He came upon a dried patch of mud and saw a hoofprint. "Someone's been here, not too long ago," he said. "On a horse."

"Who cares?" was the vinegary reply.

The path curled, and from this new angle Tom saw a slim valley between stark mountains. Long ago a titanic pile of rubble had broken away from one mountainside, slid across the gap, and nearly pinched off the dell completely. He stopped and stared because some of the boulders from the rockslide had been carried to a grassy slope and arranged on the ground to spell a message: TRESPASS AND DIE.

"Jest ignore that," the gnome said.

"But I don't want to die," Tom said softly.

The gnome chuckled. "Well, if ye do what ye're told, there's a chance ye won't. Now come on. We've got some trespassing to do."

Tom wondered what kind of being was strong enough

to write that warning, with boulders so big he could never budge them. *That creature in the dell isn't just hideous to look at*, he thought. *It's also huge. And strong.* He had to concentrate on his legs to get them moving again.

Before Tom reached the landslide, he saw something else that made him wonder. At the very end of the path, in a well-worn clearing, there was a flat slab of rock resting atop four round stones. It reminded him of a primitive altar. Beside that was a ring made of stones, with a pile of ashes and charred black sticks in the middle. As he opened his mouth to form a question, the gnome snapped, "Don't ask!"

Tom scowled and moved on, crawling, climbing, and jumping across the heap of rock. Here and there, he heard the burble of water beneath the boulders, as if a stream was entombed below. Whenever he turned around, the gnome was close behind, watching him.

He finally worked his way past the great mound of fallen rock and saw the Dark Dell beyond it, a narrow slot of green between cliffs rising sheer and gray on either side, up to lofty mountaintops a thousand feet above. A hissing sound filled the air, born from a hundred frothing streams that cascaded down the sheer walls. Tom took a deep sniff. The air was moist and mossy. And there was a hint of another scent in the misty atmosphere, barely detectable: the faraway smell of burning, or cooking.

Directly before him a shallow swamp stretched across

the throat of the valley. It wasn't terribly wide; he might have been able to hurl a stone across it. Tom took a step closer, and his foot sank through the tall grass and into muck. "It's swampy," he said, pulling his boot out with an awful squelch.

"A right genius ye are," the gnome groused.

Tom shot the gnome an annoyed look, and then eyed the soggy terrain. There were boulders scattered among it—more debris from the ancient fall—and bulging tufts of thick grass. "I can cross on those," he said, tracing a path with his gaze. He jumped to the first knoll, and then the second. When he paused to see if the gnome was following, he saw a tiny form spring out of the grass and land on his forearm. "Oh!" he cried. It was a bug of some sort. The thing was shaped like a cricket, with a thick oval body and long hind legs, poised for mighty leaps. But instead of being cricket brown or black, this creature was glassy white and almost transparent.

"You're kind of pretty." Tom thought he could see the bug's inner workings right through its outer skin. He raised his arm to take a closer look at the slender antennae, the pinhead-size eyes, and the complicated mouth with sharp, glittering mandibles that plunged abruptly into his arm.

"*Ow!*" he screamed. Tom's other hand came up by reflex and swatted at the bug, but the thing abandoned his arm with a great leap and landed in the swamp with a *plunk*. "That hurt!" He looked at the spot on his arm and saw a tiny scoop taken out of his flesh. A drop of blood welled up inside the hole. "It bit me," he said, just as another miniature stab of pain struck him on the back of the neck. He smacked himself there, but again struck only his own skin, and he heard another *plunk* in the water. When he looked at his hand, a spot of red was on the palm.

"They're eating me!" he shouted at the gnome, who only looked at the sky and puckered his lips to whistle. Tom felt another set of tiny legs grasp his ankle, and saw more of the vicious things springing out of the grass, bounding toward him. Another one bit his arm, and this time he struck fast, and felt the fat bug crackle under his open hand. Before the dead thing rolled off, he glimpsed a pinkish-red blob suspended in its glassy belly.

He felt two more land on his hair, and swatted them away. Another nip of pain flared at his ankle. A leaping bug struck him on the throat and tumbled down the neck of his shirt. Tom screamed, swiping at his clothes to knock off the dozens more that sprang at him, and he ran back the way he came, slipping off one knoll of grass and plunging knee-deep into the swamp. He felt another bite on his stomach, and mashed a fist into the spot.

Tom dashed away from the swamp, yelping with pain. He flopped on the ground and rolled onto his back to crush any bugs that might still be clinging to him, and clawed his hair with his fingers. Even when he knew the things were gone, he felt phantom creatures crawling all over his skin. Worse still, every one of the wounds began to feel like it was on fire.

Then he saw the gnome, bent at the waist and pointing at him, laughing so hard that he only produced a hoarse, gasping sound.

"You!" Tom shouted, feeling the blood in his face starting to boil. "You knew those things were there, didn't you!"

"Ha! Of course I did! How do ye like the Nippers!" the gnome cried. The smile stretched wide, and tears tumbled merrily into his beard. "I see the Nippers surely like ye!"

Tom pulled the dead, smashed bug out of his shirt and flung it to the ground. "Nippers," he muttered angrily. "You liked watching that, didn't you?"

The gnome nodded gaily, his shoulders still shuddering with laughter.

"Well, you can forget about my help," Tom said. "I'm not trying that again."

"Stupid boy," the gnome said. "Why didn't ye jest crush the glumberries and rub the juice on yer skin? That'll keep those Nippers away."

Tom goggled at the gnome. "I didn't do that because *you didn't tell me!*"

"Hoo, hoo, hoo!" The gnome slapped his knee with one hand. "Slipped my mind, I suppose!"

"Nothing *slipped*," Tom said. "You wanted that to happen." He reached for the sack of berries at his side. "Are you sure these are going to work?"

"Of course they will, ye idjit! Why do ye think I had ye pick them?"

8

The berries worked. With his skin stained purple by the juice of the glumberries, and with the sour smell clinging to him, Tom picked his way across the swamp, followed by the gnome. The Nippers still leaped at him but instantly sprang away. He was only bitten once more, on the back of his ankle just above the boot, and the gnome laughed again when he cried out in agony.

"You shouldn't laugh like that," Tom said. "It really hurts."

"Ye were lucky, piglet. What did ye get, seven or eight bites? A man can't survive more than forty or fifty. The fever kills."

"What?" cried Tom. He was suddenly aware that, besides the scorching pain in every bite, he'd broken into a sweat that sent beads of perspiration tumbling down his face. "And you let them bite me? You're cruel! And why didn't they go after you?"

The gnome sneered. "Ye'll want to pipe down pretty soon, idjit," he said. "Things dwell in the dell that ye'd best never meet."

Tom leaped from a tuft of grass to the solid ground on

the other side of the swamp, and turned to stare at the gnome. "What lives here, anyway? An ogre? A monster?"

"It's always questions with ye!" the gnome snapped, wringing his hands. "Shet yer face and keep walking!"

Tom looked around the dell. Despite its fearsome reputation, he thought it was lovely. The ground was lush with high grass and waving ferns and trees with countless vines snaking up the branches, and it was studded by blocky, house-size boulders that had broken away from the bracketing mountainsides.

A trail had been scratched through the middle of the lush greenery. When Tom stepped onto it, he froze. The hairs on the back of his neck stood at attention.

"What's the matter, dimwit?" the gnome groused.

"The trail is . . . awfully wide," Tom said. It looked like a walking path; there were no twin ruts that the wheels of a cart would leave behind. Some tall bushes grew by its side, and even ten feet high, the branches had been snapped away by something enormous that trod the path.

"Well, that's the way ye have to go. Scared, are ye?" the gnome whispered, close to Tom's ear.

"Sure," Tom replied. "I mean, who wouldn't be?" He took a deep, slow breath. "I think I'll walk next to the trail, not on it." He veered into the high brush, where he might not be seen.

Before long he'd reached the middle of the dell, and saw that the land before him had been cleared. A fence made of enormous logs sprawled from one mountainside to the other. Inside the fence Tom saw dozens of goats and sheep and cows wandering a field where the grass had been mowed low by constant grazing. And there, snug against the right-hand cliff, a huge house had been built from stone and logs and thatch. The door alone must have been twelve feet tall.

Tom instinctively hid behind a tree. The gnome stood nearby, glaring with his fists on his hips. "Well?" the gnome said.

"Well what? What am I supposed to do?"

"Go in the house, of course!"

"In there? What for?"

"I'll tell ye when ye get inside, idjit!" the gnome said.

"Listen," Tom sputtered. "If you want my help, you have to stop calling me 'idjit.'"

The gnome crossed his arms. "Fine. Let's go, dimwit."

Tom ground his teeth. "Is it safe? What if whatever lives there is still *in* there?"

"She's not," the gnome said.

"She? It's a she? How do you know?"

The gnome didn't answer. He just pointed a gnarled finger toward the far end of the dell. Tom saw, in the distance, the back of a hulking shape. It was only a blur from where he stood, partly obscured by the veil of mist thrown up by the cascading streams, but he could see a dark shaggy head atop a massive body, clad in a hooded garment. Something about the shape and size of the thing sent a cold shiver from his spine to the tips of his fingers and toes.

Whatever it was—*she* was—disappeared around a bend in the dell.

"Follow me now, unless you're too scared," said the gnome. He jogged past Tom, heading for the house with no attempt at stealth. Tom rolled his eyes toward the heavens and followed. He climbed between the horizontal rungs of the crude fence and weaved his way past the animals in the field, glancing every few seconds at the bend in the dell, in case the enormous creature suddenly reappeared.

Tom's knees went soft as he passed a muddy patch of ground scarred by a dreadfully clear footprint—long and clawed like a bear's. He could have put his own foot, heel to toe, inside it, four or five times.

"Come on, dimwit!" the gnome called back from the threshold of the house.

Tom bit his lip and ran the rest of the way. "What lives here?" he said. "What is that thing?"

"The most hideous thing ye'll ever lay eyes on, outside a mirror," the gnome said.

"Hey!" Tom replied a moment later when the barb sank in.

"Shet yer face and get inside," the gnome said.

Tom stared at the tall wooden door. Most of its surface was scratched and gouged and splintered, as if an army of lions had sharpened their claws against it.

"Strange," Tom whispered. He pressed his palms against the door and shoved, but it didn't budge an inch. *It opens outward*, Tom thought.

The doorknob was just out of his reach, so he bent his legs, sprang up, and grabbed it with two hands. With a grunt, he pulled himself up until his chin was as high as the knob. Then he put his foot flat against the wall beside the door and pushed, while using his hands to turn the knob. He heard the click of a latch, and then the door eased open with a low *creeeeak*.

Tom dropped to the ground and brushed his hands on his shirt. He looked for the gnome, hoping that his ingenuity might have earned some respect. But the little fellow was not in sight.

"What are ye waiting for, dimwit?" that screeching voice cried from inside the house. "Get in here."

Fine, Tom thought, scolding himself for expecting anything from the ill-tempered gnome. Turning sideways, he slid through the narrow gap. He held his breath, expecting to see something horrible once he was inside—piles of gnawed bones, perhaps. But it was nothing like that. He'd entered the main room of a well-kept house. It smelled wonderful. There was a stove inside with something bubbling on top in an iron pot. Bundles of herbs hung from beams that supported the thatched ceiling high above. There was a table with two chairs—much larger, of course, than any furniture he'd ever seen. *Two chairs*, Tom thought. *Are there* two *of those things around here?*

Except for the gargantuan size of the furnishings—and the fact that everything was marred by the same deep scratching and gouging that ruined the front door—it wasn't so different from the home he'd lived in with Gilbert and Joan Holly, before he had to leave the world behind and retreat to his lonely island.

"Why are we here?" he whispered. "What am I supposed to do?"

"Over there," the gnome said, jabbing his thumb toward a door against the opposite wall.

The door was ajar. Tom went to it and peered through the opening. "My goodness," he said, slipping inside.

He'd stepped into a cavern. The house, nestled against the side of the mountain, concealed an arching gap in the rock. A few rays of light entered between the roof and the cave, so there was some illumination—enough for him to see that the cave penetrated deep into the hill. Somewhere in the darkness ahead, he heard the rush of water.

"Go on—farther in. Ye'll need the glow-toad. Don't suppose ye thought of that," the gnome groused into his ear. Tom dug the jar out of the pack, pulled off the lid, and took out the toad. With the glowing, warty thing cradled against his chest, he walked into the cavern. The pale light barely reached the curving natural walls on either side. He passed a deep pool of water filled by a spring that spilled from the vaulted ceiling. He stopped to dip his cupped hands and drink. The water tasted pure and cold and sharp. The bites of the Nippers still burned, so he splashed water on them and felt a moment of relief.

Farther on, the cave grew cooler, and he crept past great barrels of food and bushels of apples. His belly groaned at the smell. He was famished, and he didn't know when he'd have the chance to eat again. But he could almost see his father cross his arms and hear his father's words: *Never steal, Tom. The man who steals only robs himself of common decency.*

Tom felt his mouth water. His hand went into his pocket, and his fingers brushed against the three coins he'd gotten from the man on the bridge. That gave him a notion. He stuffed some apples into his pack, and pried the lids off two of the barrels. There was grain in one, but salted meat in another. He stuffed some of the meat into his pack and replaced the lid. When he was done, he laid one of the coins on top of the barrel. "It's not stealing if I pay for it," he said. Beside him, the gnome sneered.

A few steps later, Tom thought he could see where the cavern finally came to an end at a wall of wet rock where drops of water trickled down like tears. Sitting by itself near the wall was something that looked like a box made of stone, no more than four feet long and three wide, with another slab of stone for a lid. In the meager light that the glow-toad cast, everything was murky and dark, but just before the wall, Tom saw something blacker still: a jagged, inky band of nothingness, as if the floor suddenly dropped away.

"That's what we're here for," the gnome said, pointing at the box. "There's something in there ye'll need. But leave the toad here," the gnome said.

"Leave it here? But I won't be able to see—"

"JEST DO WHAT I TELL YE AND PUT THE TOAD DOWN!" the gnome bellowed. "YE AND YER STUPID QUESTIONS! WHY CAN'T YE JEST DO WHAT YE'RE TOLD?"

Tom put a finger to his lips and shushed so hard that he felt spittle on his knuckle. "Are you crazy? You're the one that told me to be quiet. So stop shouting! That creature out there will hear you!"

"I'LL STOP SHOUTING WHEN YE START OBEYING!"

"Fine, fine!" Tom said. "Yeesh!" He put the toad in the jar. A green beam flew straight up through the open mouth of the jar, but no light reached the corner where the box lay. He walked toward it slowly, barely able to see. "I still don't understand why I have to do this in the dark."

"It's for yer own good, stupid boy!"

Tom kept moving. He bent at the waist and reached out with his hands, hoping to find the box in the darkness.

"Don't walk past the box," the gnome said. "Unless you want to stumble into the chasm, and go splat on the bottom." The gnome's chuckle echoed in the darkness.

"Chasm?" Tom gave some serious thought to quitting right there, but a moment later his hands found the slab that capped the box. He ran his fingers across the surface and discovered grooved lines carved into it. "I think there's writing on top."

"Never mind that!" the gnome snapped. "Ye've got to pry up that lid."

But what does it say? Tom wondered. He traced the shapes with his fingers, trying to figure out what it spelled.

"Stop that," cried the gnome. "Pry the lid!"

Tom slipped his fingers into the seam between the lid and the stone, and tugged. "It's too heavy. I don't think I can."

"Bah!" cried the gnome. "Yer hands are as weak as yer brain. Well, feel around the box. Should be a staff there somewhere."

Tom's hand came upon a sturdy piece of wood, like a walking stick, leaning against the box. "I have it."

"Then use it, ye fool! Get it in the seam and pry up the lid."

Using the staff as a lever, Tom slid the stone slab an inch at a time to one side. It worked.

"That's enough, that's enough," griped the gnome. "Ye can get yer hand in there now, can't ye?"

Tom cleared his throat before answering. "Um. Yes. What's in there?"

"Jest reach in and tell me what ye feel."

"But if you just told me what—"

"JEST REACH IN AND TELL ME WHAT YE FEEL!" roared the gnome. He was near the glow-toad, and Tom could see him batting the air above his head with oversized fists.

"All right, all right!" Tom said, gazing anxiously back down the cavern. "Keep your voice down! You'll get us killed!" He slid his hand through the narrow gap he'd made and into the black interior of the box. *I'm not enjoying this*, he thought. *Not one bit.* His shoulders crept up and the corners of his mouth headed toward his ears.

"Feel anything?" asked the gnome.

"No," Tom said. His arm was nearly elbow-deep in the box. He probed a little further. "Wait. *Yes.*" His nose wrinkled. "It feels like . . . dry moss or something." He wiggled his fingers in some fine, wiry matter that didn't resist. It may have even been falling apart under his touch. "What is it?"

"Never ye mind," said the gnome. His eyes glittered. "Jest stick yer hand into it and tell me what ye find beneath."

Tom took a deep breath and plunged his hand farther. The bristly stuff bunched up between his fingers. *I'm going to want a bath after this.* Deeper down, his hand touched something—a harder, uneven surface. "There's something under it. . . . I think it's got some kind of cloth over it."

"Right, right," said the gnome. "Now feel around for a

leather strap. Should be around there somewhere." He mimed the motion, with his hand crawling through the air like a spider.

Tom moved his hand in a widening circle, searching. His fingers brushed across a flat disk of some kind, like a coin, which seemed bound to the material. And then he came upon a thin strip of leathery material. He pinched it between his thumb and forefinger. "Got it," he said.

"Took ye long enough," said the gnome. "Make sure there's something hanging from the strap."

Tom tugged on the cord, but it seemed to be looped around an object near the end of the box. He slid his fingers along its length. There *was* something dangling at the end of the loop: something small, hard, and cold, threaded by the strap. "Yes, there's something there. It feels like . . . a key."

The gnome harrumphed. "Huzzah. Ain't ye brilliant. Now, take the strap off his head."

"Off his *head*?" Tom cried, his voice rising to a shriek. Suddenly it was all obvious: The box was a coffin, the mossy stuff was a beard, and the flat disk was a button on a shirt on the chest of a lumpy corpse. He let go of the strap and yanked his hand out so quickly that he scraped his knuckles on the lid. On another occasion he might have put the bruised skin to his lips. But not this time.

"That's *disgusting!*" he cried, stepping back from the box. And before he said another word, he heard an ominous sound come down the cavern: a loud clap that echoed off the arching stone walls before fading.

"That sounded like a door," Tom whispered. "Is the . . . creature back?"

"Maybe," the gnome replied, picking some lint off his coat. "So ye'd better do what ye're told, and quick. So I don't have to RAISE MY VOICE!"

"Shhhhhh!" Tom hissed. He looked at the box again, and felt something hot and sour bubble at the bottom of his throat, threatening to erupt. He opened his mouth and filled his lungs with the cool cavern air. Then he walked over and put his hand back in the coffin.

He found the strap once more, and pulled the loop up as far as it could go. *Please let me do this without touching the face,* he prayed. He put his other hand inside and used it to push the wiry beard down through the loop. His eyes were closed all the while, and he kept his face turned away from the musty smell creeping up from the box. Finally, he got the beard out of the loop. He tugged on the cord, imagining it passing the chin . . . the mouth . . .

The cord stopped moving. Tom moaned. He had a pretty good idea why: It was snagged on the nose. He slid the cord back toward the chest and pulled the loop up, stretching it high. This time, when he drew it to the top of the head, it came free.

Before he could pull the strap completely out of the box, something tiny and leggy crawled over the back of his hand. He tried not to scream. Only a thin squeak escaped his lips. Whatever the bug was, it jumped off his wrist when he withdrew the strap.

"Hee, hee," chortled the gnome. "Put it on, boy."

Tom looked at the dangling piece of metal that hung from the cord. "It *is* a key."

"Not jest *a* key. That's the *All-key*," said the gnome. "Put it on."

"No chance," said Tom. He tucked the strap and the key into his pocket. "Not till I wash it, anyway."

"Fine, dunderhead. So long as ye have it. Ye're going to need it." The gnome cocked his head toward the mouth of the cavern. "Uh-oh," he muttered.

"What?"

"Quill-beast," said the gnome, shrugging.

"*Quill-beast?*" whispered Tom.

A low, rumbling roar came from the creature's house. And then a strange voice: "Who's here? Who's in my house?" There were heavy footsteps, growing louder. Tom remembered the words spelled out in boulders at the entrance of the Dark Dell: TRESPASS AND DIE.

"Mind the toad," said the gnome.

Tom's eyes nearly departed their sockets as he saw the jar on the ground with a beam of green light rising up and painting the ceiling of the cavern. He ran to the jar and pressed the open end to his chest. The quill-beast had to be only a step or two from the door to the cavern. "Where should I go?" he whispered, but the gnome didn't answer.

The sides of the cavern were filled with crevices. He ran to the nearest crack in the stone and crammed himself into it, as far as he could go, just as the door was flung open.

"Who's there?" the quill-beast bellowed. It was a savage, otherworldly sound, unlike anything Tom had ever heard, like three voices mingled: growling, hissing, and clicking. "Who's sneaking about, leaving doors open? I know you're there. And I'll find you—I can see in the dark!"

Can't see me, can't see me, can't see me, Tom chanted to himself, as if that could make it true. He felt the toad hop inside the jar he cradled against his chest. Something made a high, moaning sound, and he realized it was *him*. He held his breath to make it stop, and wormed deeper into the crevice.

Footsteps drew near, thudding and scratching. An image sprang into Tom's mind: a great foot with quills on top and padded below, and wicked claws curling off the toes.

Now that he'd been inside the cavern a while, Tom's eyes had in part adjusted to the near blackness. He saw dark shapes as thick as trees swing by. *Legs.* They bristled with sharp, spiny hairs. He opened his mouth to breathe because he could hear the air whistling in and out of his nose.

Tom turned his ear to better catch every sound. The footsteps ended near the coffin and the abyss. He heard a gasp and then a crackle—a louder version of how his father's knees sounded when he squatted.

"*What?*" said the quill-beast, disbelieving. Tom heard the clatter of wood. *The staff*, he thought, realizing that he hadn't returned it to the place he found it. And then, twice, Tom heard the grind of stone against stone. Once, perhaps, to slide the lid farther off and look inside. And a second time to shove it back.

There was a sniff and a scratch. And then the strange, three-part voice again, just a saddened whisper: "Rum? Was it you, Rum? Did you come back?"

The creature lingered. The only sound she made was breathing, as deep and full as a blacksmith's bellows. *What is she doing?* he wondered. *Just staring? And who is Rum?* The toad thumped again inside the jar. *Quiet, you,* Tom thought.

Finally—finally!—the quill-beast sighed and left the cavern. Tom saw her dim shape pass his hiding place. He waited a few minutes to be safe. Then he whispered: "Hey. Gnome. Are you there?"

There was no answer. *Disappeared again. Thanks a lot.*

He squeezed out of the crevice and slid the toad's jar into his pack. Then he walked softly down the length of the cavern, back to the door. This time it was shut fast. He looked up at the knob and considered leaping for it, like he'd done at the front door. *No, too noisy.* He'd wait until the quill-beast left the house again. But who knew how long that would take?

Tom heard the creature muttering. A thin band of light seeped under the door. He got to his hands and knees and lowered his head to peer through the gap.

The quill-beast was there. Because the space was narrow, he could only see her from the waist down. She stalked the room with a pointed iron bar in one hand— a fire poker, Tom figured. He couldn't see her face, but he got a good look at the arm that emerged from her tattered sleeve. Silvery quills covered the limb, as thick as hay. The quill-beast crouched low and thrust the poker into any corners where someone might be hiding. Then she muttered something and came back toward the door where Tom was spying.

Tom leaped to his feet and ran behind the hinged side of the door just as it was thrown open. The door would have crushed him if it was swung any harder, but he'd pressed himself flat against the wall and put his hands up to slow its impact. Still, his ribs felt on the verge of snapping as he was pressed against the rock at his back.

Tom peered out from behind the door. The quill-beast stomped toward the barrels of food and started to search behind them. This was his only chance to get out, while she faced the other way. He held his breath and crept around the door and toward the threshold, taking long steps on the tips of his toes as fast as he could without making a sound.

When he was back in the house and out of her sight, he dared to breathe again. But he wasn't safe yet. His hands clenched when he realized that the door to the outside was shut fast. He couldn't leave the same way he'd come in without making a noise that would bring the quill-beast running.

He saw an open window, though, with a bench underneath. The seat might have been made for the creature to rest on, but it was chin-high for Tom. He ran to it and jumped, pushing with his hands to boost himself onto the bench. Then he swung his legs out the window, gripped the sill with his hands, and lowered himself until his arms were straight and he could drop safely onto the ground outside.

Go, he cried inwardly. He raced across the field, dodging cows and sheep, and praying the creature wouldn't burst out of the house behind him. How could he outrun those legs? His breathing was loud and hoarse, and his lungs felt like they filled with a thousand Nippers, but he kept running. He didn't feel safe until he'd clambered through the fence and disappeared into the tall brush beyond. Even then, he kept lifting his head to look back, sure he'd see the spiny monster at his heel.

When he got back to the swamp, he crushed another handful of glumberries and smeared it onto his skin. He wasn't sure if the original dose would still ward off the Nippers, but he wasn't going to take any chances. His wounds still simmered from the first attack.

Where's that gnome? Nowhere in sight, for the time being. He was sure the nasty fellow would appear again before long, with more insults flying from his lips. But for now, Tom only wanted to put as many miles as he could between himself and the Dark Dell.

This time when he crossed the swamp he was nipped only once, on the top of his head. Then he was over the landslide, past the puzzling stone altar and ring of ashes, and onto the narrow trail. Tom's shoulders ached, and he realized he'd been as tense as a coiled spring since he entered the dell. He stopped, breathed deep, and shook his arms to loosen his muscles.

The wind whistled gently in his face and carried a sound: hooves clopping, and voices speaking.

He didn't want to cause any trouble for whomever was coming, so he decided to hide. There was a stream beside the trail, another one of the countless threads of rushing water that embroidered the land of Londria. He hopped across, pushed through a dense stand of tall rushes on the other side, and hunkered down to watch in secret.

A pair of men on horseback appeared on the trail. As soon as he saw them, Tom recognized what they were and fought the urge to run.

The Marauders.

He'd never seen the invaders in person before. But they looked the way Tom always imagined they would, since his father first described them. Their hair was cut in the fashion of their tribe. Their mustaches hung low, drooping past the corners of their mouths, and their beards were plucked clean on the chin. They wore vests made from the hides of the great sheep of the mountains, and the swirling horns of rams were fastened to the helmets strung from their saddles. Their faces were scarred—not with the emblems of battle, but with ritual wounds they inflicted upon themselves when they left boyhood behind. A pair of jagged slashes started high on the temples and sloped down to meet above their noses, like savage brows. There were other scars shaped like teardrops at the outer corners of their eyes. Tom's father told him once that the Marauders carved a new tear for every person they slew.

Tom wondered if these two had been there when his mother and father's home was burned. And he wished he knew, for the thousandth time, if Gilbert and Joan Holly were still alive. He wanted to burst out of hiding and unleash his curse on this wicked pair. But first he was curious to know what they were doing here, heading straight for the Dark Dell.

One of the riders was younger than the other. His horse stepped off the trail and dipped its head toward the stream to take a drink. "Stupid beast," the young Marauder said. He pulled a short, barbed whip from his belt and raised it to strike.

"Hang on, hang on," the older one said as his horse followed the other's lead. "Let 'em drink. It's been a while. And we won't go near the water ahead, with those bloody Nippers around."

"Fine," the younger one replied with a growl. He looked disappointed as he tucked the whip into his belt. Tom noticed other things slung from the saddles: bundles of sticks, and fat jugs of dark liquid cocooned inside wicker baskets.

Tom's heart curdled with contempt. The Marauders were easily within twenty paces of where he hid, close enough for trouble to befall them. He wondered what would happen. Slowly, quietly, he let himself sink deeper behind the rushes, and found a gap where he could watch.

"Listen, now," the elder one said. "You know why Big Boss wanted you to come with me? And why we left the others back there?"

The younger one shrugged. "How should I know, Melch? I just do whatever he says. He's always right. And he's making us rich."

"Yeah, yeah," said Melch. "But he sent you for a reason. Big Boss trusts you. And he wants you to take over this job, 'cause he has other plans for me. So now you get to learn the secret."

The younger one tilted his head to one side and stared. "What secret?"

Melch reached behind him and patted one of the wicker-clad jugs. "See these? Know what's in here?"

The younger one snorted. "'Course I know. That *stuff* is in there. The anti-goat."

"Antidote, you imber-sill," Melch said, sneering. "But it ain't what you think. It's only water and wine in equal parts, with a shot of mustard seed to give it a nasty flavor."

"*That's* the antidote?"

"There *is* no antidote, don't you see? 'Cause there was never a poison in the first place."

Their voices had dropped to a whisper. Tom angled his head to catch every word of the curious conversation.

"Never a poison? I don't under—"

"You don't *have* to understand," interrupted Melch. "You just have to keep the secret to yourself. That . . . *friend* of ours can't find out about this. That would be bad. But it won't happen, because nobody knows except Big Boss, me, and now you. From here on, this is your operation. All you have to do is mix the stuff up like I told you. Then you bring the jugs to the altar and light the signal fire. Come on, I'll show you." Melch yanked on his reins, pulling his horse's head from the water. "Enough drink, you dumb beastie! Let's go."

The voices faded, along with the *clop-clop* of hooves, as the Marauders moved on toward the Dark Dell.

Tom stayed in the reeds for a while, digesting the words. *How strange. No antidote? Never a poison? What could that mean?* He wondered why nothing terrible occurred to that awful duo. They were close enough for his curse to take effect. He was sure of it. So why did nothing happen?

Maybe it did, he thought. *Maybe talking about that in front of me was unlucky for them.*

He had another notion that almost made him smile despite his jangling nerves. He'd been so scared lately of being caught by one foe or another that he'd lost the habit of saying everything out loud. *I may get killed any minute, but at least I'm not going crazy,* he thought.

CHAPTER

10

Now what? Tom had no idea what to do next. The gnome had left no further instructions before he vanished from the quill-beast's cavern.

Tom headed back down the path, away from the Dark Dell. A plume of smoke had risen in the direction of the altar a while ago, smudging the sky. Not long after that, he had to dart into the underbrush again to avoid being seen by the pair of Marauders as they returned down the path with their horses no longer burdened by the jugs or the bundles of sticks.

After they passed, Tom once more heard the voice he'd grown to hate. "Well, well. If it isn't the little outcast." The gnome was behind him, in the middle of the road, standing with his fingers interlaced and his long thumbs circling each other.

"I'm not an outcast."

"Oh, no? I must be mistaken," said the gnome, tickled to hear the fury in Tom's reply. "I thought when someone was cast out, they were referred to as—"

"I wasn't cast out!" Tom shouted. "My dad built a place for me, so I wouldn't . . ." His voice hitched and faded.

"Wouldn't what? Be a plague on mankind?" The gnome chuckled and patted his stomach with both large hands. "Smart bloke, yer dad. But he wasn't yer real dad, though, was he? And yer mum's not really yer mum?"

Tom's hands crunched into fists. Of course it was true. Everyone in Penwall knew that Gilbert and Joan Holly had found the redheaded child ten years ago, a boy hardly old enough to walk. That was during the last invasion of the Marauders, which orphaned many a child and widowed many a spouse. Gilbert and Joan, on the run themselves from the invaders, scooped up the abandoned boy and kept him safe. They never learned where Tom had come from. And Joan Holly told Tom she never really felt sorry, because she'd always wanted a son, and fate finally delivered what nature could not.

Tom always wondered about his true parents. Who wouldn't? But he'd never been ashamed of the fact that he was a lost child, taken in by good-hearted strangers. Still, he didn't care for the way the gnome had asked the question or for the nasty grin on the scoundrel's gray face.

"What do you know about that?" Tom said, seething.

"Never mind what I know, ye redheaded rat."

"It doesn't matter if they're my real mom and dad," Tom said. "They love me like their own. They take care of me."

"Oh, they took care of ye all right. I'm curious 'bout

that, actually. What happened that made yer poor folks finally decide to get rid of ye and send ye off to yer miserable shack on yer lonely island?"

Tom shut his eyes, squeezing out a hot tear. He took a deep breath, trying to stay calm. "Leave me alone," he said, tasting salt on his lips. But his thoughts flew back to that awful day—was it three years ago or four? The effect of the curse had grown worse every month. It started with minor annoyances that couldn't be explained: dinners burned, shelves collapsed, meat spoiled, milk curdled. Then it got worse. There were injuries, ever more severe. Mum twisted her ankle so many times that she never stopped limping. Dad had always been nimble with his whittling knives, but suddenly he cut himself with frightening frequency. While he waited for his fingers to heal, he couldn't carve the toys, games, utensils, candlesticks, and other wooden items that he sold in his shop. Business dwindled and hard times came with scarce money and meager food.

Gilbert and Joan didn't want to believe that the boy they'd found was the cause. But it all happened when Tom was near. The redheaded boy left misfortune in his wake wherever he went. Any child he played with ran home in tears, with fingers pinching a bloody nose or an injured hand cradled against a belly. Finally Tom had no friends at all. And the town began to point and whisper and avoid his presence. The red hair was a warning beacon, reminding everyone to stay away, far away.

Tom knew, before it was ever said, that one day he'd have to leave. He sensed the power of his curse growing, and began to feel that fluttering inside his skull whenever the bad luck was unleashed on some poor soul. One night when he was in his loft and his parents thought he was asleep, he heard them whispering. They talked about how one of them might be hurt badly one day, or even die, if things kept going the way they were. He watched them hug and heard them sob. Then they said no, no matter how bad it got, they wouldn't part with their son.

But of course it got worse. The next day, there was a fire.

It started with a strange stroke of fate. A gust of wind burst through an open window and lifted a parchment. The parchment sailed over a candle and ignited. It fluttered toward the curtains across the room, and soon they were aflame. The fire burned out of control. By the time the neighbors helped them extinguish the blaze, half the house was gone.

Standing outside the half-charred home, it was Tom who said it. *I have to get away from you. I have to leave.* The next day Tom's heartbroken father began to build the little house on the island in the stream.

The jeering voice of the gnome pierced through the haze of memory. "Poor redheaded wretch, thinking 'bout his miserable story."

Tom glared at the gnome, searching for words to put

him in his place and finding none. "What do you know about my curse, anyway? And what do you need me to do? I think it's time you told me."

"Tut, tut!" said the gnome, shaking his head. "That ain't the bargain. Remember? Ye're jest supposed to do what I tell ye."

"Right. And then you get rid of this hex."

"That's the deal, dunderhead."

Tom waved his hands in the air. "So tell me what to do!"

The gnome pointed down the road. "Suit yerself. Go that way. Take the next bridge that leads east. And get some transportation. A horse if ye can. A donkey will do."

Tom frowned back at the gnome. "Why do I need a horse?"

The gnome opened his mouth, but only a choking sound came out. He clenched his teeth and started to quake. He reached down and grabbed one of his boots with both hands, pulled it to his face, and started to gnaw on the toes.

"All right, all right," Tom cried, pressing his hands against his temples. "I'm sorry I asked another question!"

The gnome released his foot and shook his arms. The breath hissed in and out of his nose, like a furious bull's. Tom waited for the gnome to calm himself before daring another necessary, but hopefully less inflammatory, question.

"Um . . . how am I supposed to get a horse?"

The gnome crossed his arms. "Steal one, ye fool. How else?"

Tom gaped. "*Steal* one? I can't steal a horse!"

"What a strange little mouse ye are," the gnome said, curling his lip. "Then *buy* one."

Tom sighed and looked skyward. "I don't have that kind of money. I've just got the couple of coins that man gave me when I got his stuff back from the robbers."

"Hmm," said the gnome, tugging his beard left and right. He snapped his fingers. "Ha! I know! Steal the *money*!"

Tom smacked his forehead with an open palm. "For the love of—Don't you see, I can't steal anything!"

"Of course ye can," the gnome cried triumphantly, pointing at Tom's chest. "Ye have the key!"

"Huh?" Tom said. He grasped the strap from his pocket and pulled out the key. "You mean this key, from that coffin?"

"What key did ye think I meant, porridge-head?" The gnome put a hand beside his mouth and whispered: "That's a special key ye got there, boy. It's the *All-key*. It'll open any lock in the world. So ye can steal money jest fine!"

Tom shook his head. "You don't understand. It's not that I *can't* steal. It's that I *won't*. Stealing is wrong. My mum and dad didn't raise me to be a thief."

"Oh really," the gnome said sourly. "Well, some parents *they* turned out to be." He clasped his hands behind his back and paced across the path, muttering to himself.

Finally he stopped in his tracks and nodded. Then he smirked and peered up at Tom with a narrowed eye. "Listen, pea brain. What if ye *won* the money?"

"Won it? How?"

"In a game. A game of chance. A dice game, like Hazard."

"You want me to gamble?" Tom asked. He scratched his throat. "I don't know what my dad would say about that. . . ."

The gnome leaped up and down like a frog on fire, spinning in circles and punching at the sky. "WHO CARES WHAT YER DAD WOULD SAY?" he bellowed. "HE AIN'T HERE, IS HE? AND BESIDES, YER STUPID DAD AND STUPID MUM ARE PROBABLY TOO *DEAD* TO CARE!"

"Don't say that!" Tom screamed. "They're not dead! They ran from the Marauders, like everyone else!"

"Bah!" spat the gnome, waving Tom away and turning his back.

Tom rubbed his face with his hands. Now it was his turn to calm his temper. "Besides," he said, "gambling is stupid. That's what my dad always said. I'm more likely to lose than win."

"Oh really?" said the gnome, turning to face him again. The fury had left his expression, replaced by a crafty grin. "Tell me, stupid boy, if ye walk into a game of chance, and that curse of yers makes all the other players *unlucky*, what does that make *ye*?"

Tom's eyebrows wandered up his forehead, and his mouth sagged open as the answer dawned on him. "Well . . . I guess . . . that would make me . . . *lucky.*"

The gnome clapped his hands and giggled. "Yes, yes! Now, Dram isn't far from here. . . . We can be there tomorrow fer sure. Dram's a wicked place, full of wicked men. Ye're sure to find a game of Hazard there. Yes, Dram will do . . . so long as the Marauders ain't been there first."

The fire popped and crackled and flung tiny red shooting stars into the night. Tom wiggled closer to its warmth. He rubbed the arches of his feet, sore from the hours he'd walked after leaving the Dark Dell. But he was glad that the bites of the Nippers, at least, had stopped burning, and the mild fever they'd brought had finally faded away.

While they walked down the road that afternoon, and Tom ate the food he'd found in the cavern, the gnome told Tom how the game of Hazard was played. It was confusing, but Tom thought he understood it well enough to try. When they reached a crossroad, the gnome had pointed a finger in the direction of Dram and told Tom to keep walking until dark. Then, as soon as Tom's back was turned, the little fellow had vanished.

A yawn seized Tom's face and seemed to hold it forever. The inner corners of his eyes felt dry and grainy. He was tired from the day's ordeals and craved sleep, but his mind buzzed too loudly with all the mysteries he'd encountered. What was that creature in the Dark Dell? Was the key around his neck really a magical thing?

Were his mother and father alive, and if they were, how could he find them again? And what exactly did the gnome want him to do?

He heard a thump inside his pack, and remembered the glow-toad. He took out the jar, uncorked it, and turned it on its side. The soft glow of the toad beamed into the night, luring a moth almost immediately. The unsuspecting bug fluttered into the mouth of the jar. There was another soft thump, and the jar rolled a little to one side. Bits of dust from the wings of the moth floated out.

Tom sensed a presence behind him and turned around. His arms and legs jerked out of control as he saw the gnome leaning over him and staring down.

"Don't do that!" Tom said, pressing a hand against his hammering heart.

"Tut, tut," the gnome replied. "Ye scare too easy, dumb pup. Maybe ye're not up to this task after all."

Tom sat with his knees hugged to his chest. "Listen," he said, "and don't throw a fit. Can I ask one question without you losing your mind?"

The gnome inhaled theatrically and let the breath wheeze slowly out through his long nose. "Ugh. Ask me yer stupid question," he growled.

"What's your name?"

"My name? None of yer bloody business. That's my name."

"Why does all this have to be a secret?" Tom asked, his

voice cracking high. "I said I'll help you. I'll do anything if it means the end of this curse. So why can't you just tell me your name or what you want me to do?"

The gnome threw his head back and let out a long, arduous groan. His head rolled forward again and slumped against his chest. Then his face rose up with a sly sparkle in the eye.

"I'll tell you what, ye little crimson cow flop. If ye can guess my name, I'll tell ye what the task is."

"Are you serious? If I guess your name?" Tom asked. *What a weird little man you are*, he thought. He rocked back and forth for a while. "Is it Arthur?"

"No."

"Benedict?"

"No."

"Dominic?"

"No. And that's it. Ye only get three guesses a day."

"What? You didn't say anything about three—"

"IT'S MY GAME AND THOSE ARE MY RULES!" the gnome screamed, frothing at the corners of his mouth.

"You're insane," Tom said. He laid down again by the fire and turned his back to the gnome. A long time went by, and still his eyes refused to close, although his muscles ached. He looked over his shoulder and saw the gnome there, casting an ill look.

"What's the matter with you, anyway? Do you even know how to be nice?" Tom asked quietly.

The gnome glared. "What? Of course I know how to be nice, ye putrid, festering, scabby pig."

"Never mind." The fire was fading, so Tom grabbed a bundle of the fallen branches he'd collected and laid them on top of the embers. The branches were dry, so they quickly ignited. Tom watched the fire grow, sizzling and roaring. "Do you know what's strange?" he asked. "Even though you're cruel, it's nice to have someone around. You know, someone to talk to."

The gnome grunted.

"When I first moved to the island, my dad would sit on the other side of the water and tell me stories. You don't know any stories, do you?" Tom looked again at the gnome, who sat with his hands buried deep in his beard, propping up his chin.

The gnome lifted his head. "A story," he said, looking like he'd just inhaled something foul. He shifted his jaw from side to side, waggling his beard. "Ye want a story? Here's one fer ye. Once there was a bird that all the other birds hated."

Tom sat up, leaning on his elbows. "Why did the other birds hate him?"

"I don't know! Shet yer face! Ye're ruining my tale." The gnome drummed his long fingers on his knobby knees. "No, I'll tell ye why they hated him: 'Cause he was smarter and better than the rest of the birds. He'd get all the worms 'afore they did. And he'd tell the other birds how stupid and ugly and worthless they were. 'Cause it was true. So all the birds hated him, and he hated everyone right back. One day this bird flapped and flapped his wings, and flew high into the sky, as high as he could go. And do ye know what he did next?"

Tom shook his head.

"He decided to stop flying. He jest folded up his wings." The gnome crossed his arms. "And he dropped. Down, down, down, like a stone." The gnome reached up and traced a wiggly line with his finger to the ground, while he puckered his lips and made a whistling noise. When his finger touched the ground, he said, "SPLAT! Feathers everywhere. And a beak in two pieces." He put his hands behind his head and leaned back. "The end."

Tom gaped. "That's the worst story ever," he finally said.

"Hmph," said the gnome. "It's an excellent story. Didn't ye ever think 'bout that? If a bird wants to die, all it has to do is stop flapping."

Tom shook his head. "I never thought about that. Not even once."

The gnome put a fist under his chin and rested upon it. "Well, I have. Many a time."

Tom turned onto his side and leaned on one elbow. "Do you know what I think about you?"

"I don't know, what do ye think about me?" the gnome asked, mimicking Tom's high voice.

"I think you're mean because you've had a rotten life," Tom said. "I think people have been awful to you since the day you were born, and you've been awful right back to them. I think it's been going on so long, you don't even know how to be good anymore."

The gnome leaped to his feet and snarled. He loomed over Tom with his fingers curled like talons, and his lips pulled back to reveal all of his crooked, stained teeth. "How *dare* ye," he hissed. "Ye don't understand me. Ye know *nothing* 'bout me. Not a thing! Do ye understand?"

Tom was going to reply, maybe even apologize, but the gnome let out a horrible screech, jumped into the air, and dove headfirst into the fire.

"What—Are you mad?" Tom shouted. He scrambled to his feet, ready to pull the gnome out by his boots. But there was only the fire, crackling merrily, undisturbed. The gnome had vanished.

12

"Excuse me," Tom called out to the man on the road.

"Eh?" said the man, turning to squint at Tom, who stood on a hillside twenty safe paces away.

"Is that the town of Dram, over there?"

The man glanced down the road at the cluster of buildings, then back at Tom. "Yeah. It's no place for a kid like you, though."

Tom bit his lower lip. "Why not?"

"It's a town full of rats, laddie. Human vermin, that is. Rogues and villains from all over infest that place."

Yeah, that's where I'm supposed to go, Tom thought. "Thank you, sir," he said. He walked up the hill and over the crest, and then turned toward Dram, keeping the road far to his left. The farther he stayed from people, the better.

Dram was half the size of Penwall, and its hastily assembled, rickety buildings were packed even tighter. It stood at the mouth of the road that cut through the great forest, near the lawless hinterlands of Londria. This was a place to stay before one took the long road through the woods, or after one just emerged from the other side. Most of Dram's buildings were to suit the needs of travelers—inns and taverns and stables. In a back room of one of those inns, the gnome had told him, Tom was sure to find a game of Hazard. "Look for the grimiest, shadiest place in town," the gnome had said, rubbing his hands together with glee.

Tom heard a rolling boom in the distance. There were dark clouds on the horizon, flashing with inner light. As he paused to watch, he saw them boil toward the heavens, blotting out the blue. A cool breeze whooshed over the hills and ruffled the green skirts of the willows. The sleepy trees awoke, and their branches shrugged and lifted like marionettes stirring to life. Tom was glad to be near a town, where he might take refuge if the storm came this way.

There weren't many people outside, so Tom stepped into the middle of the road and walked, looking for an inn or tavern. A woman bustled out of a doorway on his left, carrying a dead, featherless chicken by the feet, so Tom veered right, putting as much space between them as he could. He pressed himself against the wall on the other side of the road. The smell of coal and smoke came to his nose, and he heard the rhythmic hammering of metal on metal inside the wall. *A blacksmith*, he figured. A moment later the hammer struck something softer than iron, and the hidden blacksmith screamed and unleashed an astonishing combination of words that Tom had never heard before in all his sheltered years. *Sorry*, he thought, stepping away from the building.

When he looked back at the wall, he saw that it was covered with papers tacked up for all to read. They were notices about rewards offered for the capture or death of criminals. Most of the posters merely featured the names of the wanted men, a list of their crimes, and a few words about their appearance. But one was different. Tom's feet slowed to a halt, and he wavered where he stood, staring at something he could hardly believe. He went closer, feeling unsteady, and finding it difficult to propel himself forward through the air.

The poster that caught his eye was older than the rest, tattered and yellowed. A strong breeze could tear it to pieces and bear the shreds away like autumn leaves. Below its words, the poster featured a drawing in silhouette. While it only represented the black shadow of a being, it bore a startling resemblance to the gnome, with sticklike arms and legs, oversized hands and feet, and a large head topped by a floppy, pointed hat.

Tom tried to swallow, but there was no moisture in his throat. He read the hand-lettered words:

REWARD

300 GOLD PIECES

FOR THE CAPTURE OF THE FIEND

RUMPEL–STILTSKIN.

WANTED FOR CRIMES AGAINST KING AND KINGDOM:

THIEVERY, POACHING, SPYING, SORCERY, SWINDLING,

TRESPASSING ON AND DESECRATING THE PROPERTY OF THE KING,

THE ATTEMPTED ABDUCTION OF THE QUEEN'S INFANT SON,

AND OTHER NOTORIOUS DEEDS.

BEWARE—THIS VILLAIN CAN VANISH AT WILL

A thin, wheezing voice spoke up behind Tom. "Know anything about that one, boy?"

Tom saw a short, gaunt man who must have stepped out of another door nearby. The man didn't look well; he was bent at the waist and his legs were so bowed he could have straddled a barrel without touching it. His hands were busy scratching at his thin, gray hair.

Tom took an instinctive step back. "I have a bad cold, sir. You better not come too close."

The fellow took a step back of his own. "Well, I don't need to be no sicker than I already am. But three hundred gold pieces can cure a lot of ills, eh?" He jabbed a quivering thumb toward the sheet. "You had a funny look on your face when you saw that picture. You seen that rascal? Maybe I can help you catch him!"

Tom tugged at the collar of his shirt. "Uh. Nope, never seen him, sir. And, uh . . . never heard of him, either." *Tom, you're the worst liar ever,* he bemoaned to himself.

"Never even *heard* of him?" the man said. He stopped scratching his hair and went to work on his chest, raking it with his fingers. "Well, old Patzer was just kidding you anyhow, boy. Nobody's seen old Rumpel-Stiltskin for years, far as I know."

Tom stared at the poster. His stomach twisted as he read the long list of misdeeds for the second time. One troubled him above the others. He turned back to look at Patzer. "Abduction of the queen's infant son? Did he really do that?"

Patzer grinned. "Now that's a famous incident. Can't believe you never heard that one! Happened a long time ago, farther south, right under the nose of the king. Of course, this was two or three kings ago! My mother used to tell me the story." There was a railing in front of the inn, and Patzer leaned on it, settling in to tell the tale. While he spoke, he finished scratching his chest and moved on to his belly, thighs, neck, and a place or two that made Tom grimace and turn his head in the other direction.

"Back then, there was a miller who loved to make silly boasts about his daughter, Helena," began Patzer. "One day he said that Helena was so talented with the spinning wheel, she could spin straw into gold. This boast came to the king's ear, and the king said, 'Oh really? Then bring this lass to me, and make her prove it.'

"Now the miller was in a fix, because King Berold was cruel, greedy, and mad, all at the same time. Berold said he'd put the girl to death if she couldn't produce the gold, and marry her if she could! Things looked grim for

Helena. But then this strange little man appeared out of nowhere and offered to use his magic to spin the gold. The little man had one condition, though: He wanted her firstborn child in exchange. What could Helena do? Death was the only alternative, so she agreed, hoping to later find a way out of the bargain.

"Well, the king got his gold, and he made the miller's daughter his queen. And soon enough, a son was born, the new prince of Londria. And guess who showed up, demanding that the newborn prince be turned over? The strange little man, of course. Queen Helena moaned and wept, and then the little man proposed a cruel game of his own: If Helena could guess his name within three days, she could keep the baby. Well, Helena made many guesses, none of them right. But a miracle saved her, because on the third day, a servant told her that he'd come upon a strange man in the middle of the woods, dancing by firelight and singing—and the fellow had sung out his own name: *Rumpel-Stiltskin*! So when the little man came to claim the child, she guessed his name straightaway. And Rumpel-Stiltskin vanished, just like that."

Tom covered his mouth with his palm and exhaled, feeling warm breath from his nose on the back of his hand. *What a strange story*, he thought. His thoughts tumbled inside his head. He remembered what the creature in the Dark Dell had said: *Rum? Was it you, Rum? Did you come back?* Was that Rum the same fellow as this

Rumpel-Stiltskin? He glanced at the list of crimes on the sheet again, and wondered if he should really be helping such a dangerous character. Surely the gnome was up to no good. Why should Tom do this mysterious task for him, even if it meant the end of his curse?

Then he remembered: The gnome had promised to tell him what the task was if Tom could guess his name. But there was no reason to guess anymore. Tom smiled, looking forward to the moment he would surprise the gnome with his name. *Rumpel-Stiltskin!*

That sealed it. Tom would go along with the plan for now. "Excuse me, sir," he said to Patzer. "Do you know if there's a game of Hazard being played anywhere in this town?"

Patzer's eyes widened and he straightened up from his slouch. "Hazard? What's a little boy like you want with a game of Hazard?"

"If you take me there, I'll make it worth your time. If I win."

"Will you, now?" Patzer smirked, spat again, and wiped his sleeve across his spattered chin. "Then follow me, lad. Follow me!" Another boom of thunder rolled across the land. Patzer peered up at the dark clouds drifting toward the town. "We'd best get inside, anyway."

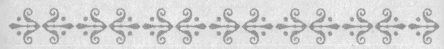

13

Tom followed Patzer into the back of a dingy tavern. As he passed through the open door, he was sure he felt something moving inside his shirt, like a beetle scrabbling against his chest. For a moment he thought it might be a Nipper that had stayed hidden in a fold of his shirt all this while. He slapped at the spot, and winced with pain as something hard and sharp cut into his flesh.

It wasn't a beetle at all. It was the key he'd retrieved from the stone coffin in the Dark Dell. *Weird*, he thought. He was sure it had moved. He pulled it out from beneath his shirt and stared. The shape was different, he was certain of that. It was longer and thinner than when he'd found it. He noticed a lock on the door he'd just passed through, and remembered what the gnome had told him: *That's a special key ye got there, boy. It's the All-key. It'll open any lock in the world.*

"Well?" said Patzer. Tom's head snapped up, and he saw the man staring at him, waiting.

"I'm coming," Tom said, tucking the key back under his shirt. They passed through a poorly lit dining room with tables for travelers. The room stank of sausage and sweat and ale. Tom cringed as a man with a tray full of mugs walked past him, far too close. The fellow tripped over nothing that Tom could see, and dowsed a table full of brutes with the frothy contents of the mugs. He heard the sounds of scuffling in his wake and the plaintive apologies of the server.

Patzer chuckled at the mess. He led Tom out of the dining hall and into a dark hallway in the back, giving his hindquarters a vigorous scratching as he walked. Tom followed many paces behind and waited at a distance as Patzer knocked on a closed door.

The door creaked opened a crack, and a thin slice of a leery face peered out.

"Hullo, Bishop. I got someone who wants in," Patzer said.

The eye in the crack glanced at Tom and turned back to Patzer. "A *boy?* Are you joking, Patzer, you flea-bit fool?" Bishop said.

"I have money," Tom said. He held up his palm, showing the coins.

"Hmph," said the voice from behind the door. "That'll last you a throw or two, if you're lucky. Where's your folks, sonny?"

"I . . . I don't know," Tom said. "They ran from the Marauders. Back in Penwall."

"That so?" The voice of Bishop sounded pleased. The eye narrowed, looking Tom over from head to toe. Tom felt like a lamb being appraised by a wolf. *Wonder if I shouldn't have told him about my parents.* His nerves jangled, and he might have turned and run if the door didn't swing open right then.

He saw the rest of Bishop: a scruffy, stony face on a short-necked, thick-shouldered body. "I suppose you can play if you want. Get in here."

Tom hesitated, keeping his distance. Fortunately Patzer spoke for him.

"The boy doesn't like to get too close. Says he's got a cold. Doesn't want to get anyone sick."

Bishop flashed a dark grin. "That so? Well, then." He took a few steps back and swept his arm in a formal gesture. "After you, boy."

Tom walked into the room, moving swiftly past Bishop and stepping into the open space. *Don't let anything happen yet*, he pleaded silently. He clenched his teeth as if that could trap the curse inside. His gaze darted around, taking in his surroundings.

There were maybe two dozen men in the room. Tom could tell at a glance who'd been winning and who'd lost their hard-earned wages. The winners—there were less of those—stood straight and tall, bobbing their heads and bouncing on their heels. Their faces were flushed with triumph, and they spoke avidly to the men around them. Tom could see that they were not yet satisfied. Whatever they won was not enough. They were hungry, greedy for more, rocking their weight from foot to foot and licking their lips at the thought of more—*more*.

The losers were haunted and desperate. Their faces were drained of color, with shadows in their eyes. They didn't speak at all. They slouched or leaned on the sturdy wooden pillars that supported the roof, souls trampled by defeat. Their gazes fell to the planks of the floor, or rose pleading to the angled ceiling above. And their hands constantly fidgeted—tugging at sleeves, rubbing eyes, pinching hair, and clasping one inside the other.

From the corner of his eye, Tom noticed something strange. Among the crowd, one man, taller than the rest, turned away and shielded the side of his face with his hand. Tom watched the man, sensing something familiar. But the man pushed his way to the back of the crowd and lowered himself, perhaps sitting. Then Tom couldn't see him at all.

The rest of the players stared at Tom, and their disapproval and resentment rushed over him like a cold wave. This was the saddest room he'd entered in his life, and he couldn't wait to leave. It was a relief when their attention went back to the wooden table in the middle of the room, where the game of Hazard was played.

The table was waist-high and round, raised at the rim to keep the dice from falling to the floor. A short, jowly man sat on a tall chair at the far end, above the others. *He's the groom-porter*, Tom thought, remembering the word the gnome—Rumpel-Stiltskin—had taught him. *The groom-porter calls out the odds.*

There was a man standing at the near end of the table, shaking his cupped hand. Tom heard the rattle of dice in the loose grip. *It's his turn,* Tom thought. *He's the caster.*

The man rolled the dice. When they stopped tumbling, the others around the table cheered, and the man's shoulders slumped. He turned and walked away, staring with glassy eyes, and the man to his left eagerly scooped up the dice.

"Give the boy a turn!" called out a wheezy voice. It was Patzer, grinning and scratching each shoulder with the nails of the opposite hand.

"Why, Patzer? Is he itchin' to play?" shouted Bishop. The winners howled with laughter, and the losers smiled wanly. Patzer grinned and scratched himself even more vigorously.

"Sure, why not?" the groom-porter grumbled. "Let little red top have his turn. Get this farce over with!"

The man with the dice held the pair of bone-white cubes out to Tom.

Tom stayed back and cleared his throat. "Um . . . just put them on the table, sir, if you please."

All around the room, the men exchanged smirks and raised eyebrows. Tom heard chuckles and whispers. The man with the dice shrugged and dropped them onto the rim of the table and stepped aside.

Tom approached the table with small, wary steps. He

was too close to everyone, there was no doubt about it. Still, even after living with his curse for so many years, he could not exactly predict how it would work. He hoped it would express itself now in the simplest and least violent way: by spoiling their game of chance.

"What's your main, lad?" the groom-porter said.

"My main? Oh, right," Tom said. The gnome had informed him about this step. *Ye might have to roll fer it, or ye might jest have to tell them.* "I choose seven, sir."

"Seven's the main!" cried the groom-porter for all to hear.

Tom picked up the dice, rattled them, and brought his hand back to cast. All around him, men gasped.

"Hold on, boy!" shrieked the groom-porter, even as Tom froze in place. "What's your wager?"

Tom knew his face had just turned redder than his hair. "Sorry," he said. He dug into his pocket where he had the two coins. He put them on the table. A moment later other men placed their own bets, equaling the value of the coins Tom had put down. Tom looked up at the groom-porter with a wince. "That's my wager. Do I roll now?"

The groom-porter scowled and nodded.

Tom cast the dice. They clattered and tumbled and rolled to a stop, and a chuckle echoed around the table. Tom stared at the result, and swallowed hard. It wasn't what he expected. Both dice showed a single dot on top. He'd rolled a two.

"Alas, the eyes of the snake!" shouted the groom-porter, grinning. "Two's the chance! Seven's the main!"

Tom knew what this meant. A two was the worst roll a person—an *ordinary* person—could cast. To win now, he had to roll a two again, *before* he rolled a seven. And of course the odds against that were great. With a pair of dice, there was only one combination that would produce a two: a pair of single dots. But there were three ways to roll a seven: with a four and a three, a five and a two, and a six and a one.

"Three to one!" called the groom-porter. Tom saw more bets placed around the table, according to the odds the groom-porter had just named.

Whether it was the custom of these men, or the curse at work, or the fact that Tom was just an innocent boy out of place in this seedy room, all the bets were against him. The groom-porter used a long stick that looked like a tiny hoe to push the dice back toward him. Tom picked up the dotted cubes and shivered, feeling the sensation he'd known before: a gentle ruffle on his brain, like wind in the rye. He cast the dice with little doubt about what would turn up.

There were gasps everywhere and guffaws from the men who hadn't bet. "He nicked it!" someone shouted.

Whatever that means, Tom thought. He knew only that he'd rolled another pair of ones.

An appalled quiet filled the room. The bettors watched in dismay as their coins were raked away and shoved in front of Tom, along with the dice. Tom watched with a pinched feeling in his belly as more men put down wages, stubbornly betting against him once more. *If only they knew*, Tom thought. He gathered up the dice.

"You're betting it *all?*" asked the groom-porter, leaning forward with one eyebrow an inch higher than its companion. "On those odds?"

"Yes, sir," said Tom. He waited for all the bets to be placed, and cast the dice again. When they tumbled to a stop, he heard the sharp intake of breath from all around, followed by a moment of utter silence.

"Nicked it *again!*" someone moaned.

More coins disappeared from the circumference of the table, and Tom's pile tripled in size for the second time. Tom stared down at the mishmash of coins. *Enough for a horse? I need to be sure.* He gathered the dice again.

"He'll never do it three times," grumbled a one-eyed man, slapping down another bet. "It ain't possible. Never three." The others around the table did the same. Tom could feel their animosity, scorching him like the sun. The men drifted closer, fixing their eyes on him. Tom didn't touch the pile of coins in front of him. He nodded to the groom-porter, who simply shrugged. With trembling hands Tom threw the dice again. They clattered, rolled, bounced off the far edge, and tumbled back. When they came to a rest, another pair of black dots stared unblinking at the ceiling.

"Two," the groom-porter said quietly, in disbelief.

"No!" bellowed the one-eyed man. His fist came down hard on the table, causing the pile of coins to shift. The dice hopped and rolled, and still came down showing a pair of ones.

That's definitely enough, Tom thought, eyeing the mountain of coins that was pushed before him. "I'm done, sir," he said to the scowling groom-porter. His voice squeaked as he added, "Thank you all very much!" He smiled, hoping that would help, and gathered up the coins as swiftly as he could. It took an alarmingly long time. He filled one pocket, then another, and still had too many coins left. So he shrugged off his pack and stuffed them inside as fast as he could, raking them in with his forearm. A few coins missed the opening and rolled noisily around the floor, and he didn't bother to go after them. When he glanced up, he saw the faces of the men who'd lost so much this day and probably many days before. The question was in their eyes: *Why? Why were you lucky? Why not me?*

Tom caught a hint of motion behind him and heard the door close. Someone had slipped out of the room. He picked up the pack and hugged it to his chest. His heart was thudding and he blinked madly. "So long, now. Thank you again," he said, edging backward toward the door.

"Hold it!" shouted the one-eyed man. Tom was going to run, but Bishop blocked the door with his broad body.

"Check the dice," the one-eyed man demanded. "Nobody rolls like that! He must have cheated! He switched the dice on us!"

"Yes!" cried the others, murmuring to each other.

The groom-porter picked up the dice and inspected them. "They look like mine," he announced.

"Cut 'em open!" demanded another man in the crowd, one of the heaviest bettors. The groom-porter nodded. He reached under the table and pulled out a huge butcher's knife. With a crowd like this, Tom wasn't surprised that such a weapon was kept handy. The groom-porter put one of the dice in front of him. With his tongue sticking out of the corner of his mouth, he lined the rectangular blade up over the die and brought the knife down. The one-eyed man leaned in close, keen to see the results.

Tom flinched, fully expecting his curse to have some awful effect, and horrified to think that the groom-porter might miss and lop off his own fingers. But instead the knife struck the die perfectly, cleaving it in two. One piece remained on the table, and the other shot into the open mouth of the one-eyed man, who clutched his throat and started to choke, with his eye bulging from its socket.

The groom-porter inspected the remaining half as the others gathered near, squinting. "Nothing amiss here, gentlemen," the groom-porter said. "The boy won fair and square."

Not exactly, Tom thought. Somehow this felt as bad as stealing. But it was done. "Good-bye, then," he said. He headed for the door with his pack clutched against his chest as someone starting thumping the one-eyed man on the back, trying to dislodge the broken die.

Tom stepped outside the inn and filled his chest with air. It felt as if he'd held his breath the entire time he was in that awful room playing that terrible game. He thought for a moment that hours had passed instead of minutes, because it was as dark as dusk. When he looked up he saw that the storm clouds had arrived, obscuring the afternoon sky. A boom of thunder shook the town, and the air smelled wet.

"Now, where can I buy a horse?" Tom wondered aloud, looking down the street. The blacksmith might be the right person to ask, he figured, if he was in the mood to answer questions after his recent injury. He went back in that direction, but stopped when he heard Patzer calling to him from behind.

"Boy! Boy!" Patzer cried, hobbling toward him on bowed legs. He stopped a few strides away when Tom raised his hand as a warning to keep his distance. "Don't go that way!"

"Why not?" Tom asked, wiggling his shoulders into the straps of his pack. He heard the coins jingle inside and felt their weight tug at his pockets.

"Ambush," Patzer whispered with his hand beside his

mouth. "Someone saw you win all that money. He's waiting for you down the road."

Tom looked down the way that Patzer pointed. *Great,* he thought, biting his bottom lip. "I need to find a stable or something," he told Patzer. "Someone to sell me a horse or a mule."

"Here's what you do," Patzer said, scratching behind an ear. "See that alley there, 'tween those buildings? Go down there. It's tight at the end, but you can get through. Turn left, and you'll see the back of the nearest stables at the other end of town. And you'll avoid that rotter who wants to rob you!"

Tom smiled. "Thank you!" But before he could go, something on the other side of the road, high on a peaked roof, captured his attention. It was the unmistakable figure of the gnome—*Rumpel-Stiltskin,* Tom reminded himself—silhouetted against the stormy sky. The gnome was leaping up and down and waving his pointed hat in the air.

"What are you looking at, young fellow?" asked Patzer.

"Er" was all Tom could think of to say. He watched Patzer turn to look in the direction of the gnome, but Rumpel-Stiltskin was gone. "Just the clouds," Tom said.

Patzer gave him a strange look. "Well . . . you're a lucky one, young fellow. You ought to play Hazard more."

I'd rather have a hundred Nippers poured down my pants, Tom thought. He dug into his pocket and fished out one of the coins. "Thanks for all your help, sir. Here!" He tossed the coin to Patzer, who pawed at it but missed. The coin struck him in one eye. Patzer yelped and clapped a palm over the side of his face.

Tom groaned. "Sorry!" he called back as he ran for the alley.

The alley was ripe with a sickly stink, as if rats crawled there to die. It narrowed and darkened as the lopsided walls of the buildings closed in. The storm blew a fresh gust of cold wind down the narrow space, sending dry leaves up into corkscrew flight. Tom saw just a narrow band of sky above, and the churning cloud flickered when he glanced up.

Tom's breath seized up inside his chest. The end of the alley was sealed by a tall fence. When he turned around, he saw men at the mouth of the alley, blocking his escape. They walked halfway down and paused, spreading out in a line across the breadth of the space.

With bitterness frosting his heart, Tom saw that one of the men was Patzer. "Sorry, lad," Patzer said with his injured eye squeezed shut. "But that's quite a pile of money you won."

Tom recognized a few of the others from the room where the game was played. When he saw the tall man among them, he realized who it was that hid his face and snuck out of the room. It was Toothless John, the robber from the forest.

The last time Tom saw him, Toothless had run his face into the trunk of a tree. Now his nose was mashed and purple and pushed to one side, and the robber had heavy black crescents under his eyes. "How lucky for me," Toothless said—although with his ruined nose, it sounded like "Ow luggy vor be.""Running into you here. Glad I had the urge for a game of Hazard!"

"You should leave me alone, all of you," Tom said. He hoped the men didn't notice his legs shaking. "Really. Don't come near me."

"No need, lad," Patzer said. He glanced up at the boiling black sky. "Let's make this quick, before we all get soaked in this storm, eh? Just toss us the money. Do that right away, and Toothless here won't hurt you."

"Yes, I will," Toothless growled. He pulled a long, lethal-looking knife from his belt. "You were lucky last time, you red runt. I won't miss you again." He flipped the knife, caught it by the blade, and raised it high behind one shoulder. Toothless pointed with the other hand, right at Tom's chest. The robber flashed a grin without teeth, and arched his back.

An instant later a man was dead.

There was an indescribable explosion of thunder that shredded the air, and rang every bone in Tom's body. He screamed and leaped and clapped his hands over his ears. Before his eyes instinctively shut themselves, his mind was seared by a terrible sight. A brilliant, white-hot vein of fire and light poured down from the sky and into the knife that Toothless held. There was flame and steam, and Tom was sure he'd seen the villain's eyes turn as bright as the sun. The men to the left and right of Toothless were knocked onto the ground by some unnatural force.

Tom lay in the alley with his knees pressed against his chest and his arms covering his face. He slowly raised his head and looked at his attackers. Toothless John was flat on the ground, a smoldering corpse, undeniably dead. Mercifully he'd fallen facedown into the dirt. His boots had been blown off his feet. A charred hand still gripped the knife. The rest of the gang was scattered around Toothless, in a daze.

Tom looked away as he wobbled to his feet on ground that seemed to rise and fall like the ocean. His throat felt as if it was being squeezed by a powerful grip. He opened his mouth and forced down a breath, and it came back up again in a choking sob.

"I never wanted to hurt anyone," he said. "I didn't mean to."

"You . . ." It was Patzer. He'd struggled to his knees, and pointed a finger at Tom. "You *made* that happen. . . . It was sorcery! Witchcraft!"

"No," Tom said. He started walking, then running. The men who'd come to their senses crawled out of his path, gritting their teeth and holding their palms out to ward him away, as if Tom might send another bolt of lightning down upon them.

Tom ran unsteadily out of the alley. He rushed down

the street, weaving to avoid contact with the few people who were still outside. He shouted "Stay away!" when someone came too close. The storm was still overhead, rumbling and igniting, blotting out the sky, and he was terrified that another bolt would kill another person, someone entirely innocent this time.

A fat drop of rain struck his forehead. He heard the patter of more drops, only a few at first, then the tempo hastened until it turned into a hiss of hard rain. He kept running down the street, afraid to go into any of the shops or inns to escape the storm. Was there really a stable at the end of town, a place where he could buy a horse? If there was, maybe he could also find an empty barn where he could hide during the downpour.

Ahead of him, at the far end of town, he heard a scream. Then another. Then a chorus of shrieks. He stopped in the middle of the street and stared through the rain, wiping the drops out of his eyes and making a brim with his hands.

There was another cry in the distance that struck his heart like a frozen spear. It wasn't human. It was a strange, alien, complex howl. He'd heard something like it before. But from where?

The Dark Dell.

A boy about his age ran down the street. Tom stepped out of his way to let him pass. The boy turned with enormous eyes and shouted to Tom: "Run! The Marauders are here—and their creature!"

It's me, Tom thought. *I've brought bad luck to the whole town.* "The curse is getting stronger," he whispered.

The road was straight, and he could see to the far end of Dram, where a hill rose up beyond the border. There was a sound that he thought was thunder at first. But then he saw the Marauder army pour over the crest of the hill. There were hundreds on horseback and hundreds more on foot. Oily black smoke spiraled toward the sky from the countless torches they held high. The helmets, adorned with the curling horns of rams, made them look like a host of demons.

The rain came to an abrupt stop. All around Tom, people emerged from the buildings that lined the street. The men of Dram were not the type to back down from a confrontation. They came with swords and clubs, axes and pitchforks, ready to fight. They stared at the invaders with narrowed eyes, jutting jaws, and sneering lips.

Another one of those terrible animal howls filled the air. Tom watched the center of the line of horsemen part, leaving a gap in the middle. Something enormous rose up from the other side of the hill, passed through the gap, and ran at a ferocious speed toward the town. It was covered with a cloak, a hood drawn tight around the face.

The size, the shape, the way it moved . . . Tom had seen something like it before. The quill-beast of the Dark Dell. *But she wasn't this big,* he thought.

Clawed hands with leathery palms came out of the cloak. Like the beast in the Dark Dell, this one had a shaggy coat that bristled with thousands of terrible, sharp needles. The quill-beast's hands reached up and pushed back the hood that covered its face. Tom turned away the instant he glimpsed what was under the hood, but it was too late to keep the panic from flooding his body.

Around him everyone screamed. Men shrieked like babies and threw their weapons to the ground. Most of them turned and fled up the street, and others dove into buildings. One bug-eyed man pulled his own hair out by the roots as he ran.

Tom heard his kneecaps rapping against each other. His breath raced, and he felt the pulse of his heart in his neck, his legs, his hands, his ears. *That face,* he screamed inside. *That horrible face!*

He heard footsteps all around him, doors and windows slamming, weeping and shouting. *Move,* he urged himself. But the muscles in his legs had turned to sludge, and he dropped to his knees.

The ground under his feet trembled with a growing rhythm: *whump, whump, whump, whump, WHUMP, WHUMP!* The creature was coming near. Tom could only stare at the road because if he looked up and saw the face again, he knew that fright would make him faint.

He saw the light of the sun fall on the ground as the storm clouds drifted away, a strange sight for such a dark moment. The steps grew louder, and every time they came down, they jolted his body. A shadow grew in the dirt on the street, like a flood of ink, and washed over

Tom. The footsteps stopped. He heard a snort and felt a warm breath on his shoulders. The quill-beast was standing over him. *I'm going to die now,* he thought. *I wanted to cure my curse and find my parents. But instead I'm going to die in this street.*

That strange voice boomed out, three horrors in one: the growl of a wide, wet throat; the click of gnashing teeth; and the hiss of a serpent's tongue, intermingled in terrible harmony. It was deeper than the voice Tom had heard in the Dark Dell. "Fools! Run, all of you! Run or face me!"

The creature howled again, so loud that it rivaled the crack of thunder when Toothless John died. Tom screamed into his hands, but he couldn't even hear his own cry.

"You—boy!" It was the quill-beast, hissing down at him. Tom could hear the countless needles that covered its body bristling and tearing at the garment the creature wore. "Do you want to die? Run while you can. Do you hear me? Run!"

Tom crunched his eyelids together. His hands shook madly, but he managed to press his palms to the ground and push himself up onto his feet.

"NOW!" screamed the quill-beast, and Tom was suddenly in command of his legs again. He sprang up and ran as fast as he could to the far end of town with his arms thrown up in front of his face. Behind him he heard the thunder of hooves, and he knew the army of Marauders was coming to plunder and burn.

CHAPTER

15

Tom ran, nearly blind with fear, past the last of the buildings as people shouted and wept and fled the town on horseback, donkey, cart, or foot, carrying what they could. Even in his panic, he knew he had to keep his distance from the others so his curse did not compound their misery. Leaving the road, he ran into the forest that bordered Dram.

He raced past trees, using his hands to ward off the branches in his path, tripping over roots and rocks until he couldn't run anymore, and he collapsed on the ground.

Why didn't it kill me? Why did it let me go? As he wondered those things, the image of that terrible face invaded his brain again.

The face! It was complicated and grotesque, as if spawned from a nightmare. The face was bloated, wrinkled, and ghastly white, with angry purple veins coursing just under the surface and wreathed by those deadly quills. The eyes were bulging orbs that flickered with inner fire. The mouth was a gaping, misshapen crevice with fangs on the end of knobby, articulated joints, and a quivering, forked tongue. Writhing tentacles hung like whiskers from the pointed chin. The flesh below the chin ballooned and contracted with every terrible scream that the creature unleashed.

Tom groaned and mashed the heels of his hands into his eyes, trying to erase the vision. And then he heard a familiar chuckle, coming from somewhere over his head. He looked up and saw the gnome sitting on the branch of a tree, swinging his long feet back and forth.

"Haw, haw! I tried to warn ye, but now I'm glad ye were too dumb to notice! That was quite a show ye put on! A stroke of genius, it were!" The gnome must have thought he said something terribly clever, because he threw his head back and roared with laughter.

"It isn't funny," Tom said.

The gnome hopped off the branch and landed on the ground as nimbly as a squirrel. He smoothed his wrinkled coat and shook his head. "Could've fooled me. But never mind that. I presume ye won at Hazard?"

"Yes, I won. But the Marauders came before I could get a horse."

"Never mind," said the gnome. "Ye don't need it."

Tom stared. "What? Why not?"

The gnome pursed his lips and fiddled with one of the broad buttons on his jacket. "Change of plans. No need for a horse anymore."

Tom stared some more, with his jaw hanging slack. "No need for a . . ." he sputtered. *That's enough*, he thought. "I did all that for *nothing*? A man got killed by lightning for *nothing*?"

"Yeah, I saw that." The gnome chuckled. "Ye know what yer trouble is, boy? No sense of humor."

Tom felt like his head was going to explode. "That's enough, you wicked, horrible, awful little man!" he shouted. "I want to know what it is you want me to do! Right now!"

The gnome smirked and folded his arms. "Don't ye remember? I said I'd tell ye if ye can guess my na—"

"*Rumpel-Stiltskin!*" interrupted Tom, stabbing a finger near the gnome's face.

The gnome made a choking sound and clapped his enormous hands over his mouth. His eyeballs rolled wildly in their sockets. He grabbed the brim of his hat and twisted it back and forth with his cracked teeth grinding together. "WHAT?" he bellowed. "YE DIDN'T SAY THAT!"

"Yes, I did," said Tom, enjoying a rush of triumph. "Your name is Rumpel-Stiltskin! I guessed your name, so now you have to tell me."

Rumpel-Stiltskin groaned through his clenched teeth. He leaped up and stomped the ground. Then he seized one arm with the other and started to wrench it back and forth with such fury that Tom bit his lip and waved his hands in the air.

"Calm down," Tom cried, wondering how those arms—so frail that the gnome had reinforced them with wooden splints and leather straps—could handle the violent tugging. "You're going to hurt your—"

Tom cut himself off with a shriek. There was a loud snap, and the tearing of thread, and the gnome's spindly arm came right out at the shoulder. It spun in the air, still clad in the torn sleeve, and landed on the ground near Tom's feet. Rumpel-Stiltskin stared at it, surprised at first, and then annoyed. Next he glared up at Tom. "That was *yer* fault," he said, pointing at Tom with his remaining hand.

"*My* fault?" Tom mumbled into the palm that covered his mouth. He watched with horror as the fingers on the loose arm started to move. The hand crawled across the ground toward the gnome, dragging the rest of the arm behind like an unwieldy tail.

"Ye didn't see that," Rumpel-Stiltskin said. He picked up the arm and tried for a moment to shove it back into his shoulder, as if it might pop back into place. When that didn't work, he muttered something unpleasant and stuffed the limb down the front of his shirt.

Tom's stomach threatened to pipe its contents, volcano-like, up his throat. "How come you're not bleeding?" he asked weakly.

"Ye and yer stupid questions," muttered the gnome, turning his head and scowling into the distance. "How did ye learn my name?"

"That doesn't matter," Tom said, taking deep breaths. "You have to tell me what the task is. That was the bargain."

"Fine." Rumpel-Stiltskin snorted. "Though ye'd have figured out what I want by now if ye didn't have maggots where yer brains ought to be." Tom watched with dismay as the lump under the gnome's shirt wiggled and rose until the fingers of the missing arm poked out of the collar and grabbed hold of Rumpel-Stiltskin's beard. The gnome grimaced and pried the fingers loose, swatting at the hand until it retreated meekly out of sight.

"I wanted ye to go find the Marauders," he said once he'd composed himself. "But now the Marauders have come to ye. So ye don't need the horse anymore, do ye, genius?"

Tom shook his head in disbelief. "The *Marauders*? Why did you want me to find the Marauders?"

"Simple," said Rumpel-Stiltskin. "Ye see, there's something strange going on with that tribe. I know that bunch, and before this they were never worth spit as warriors. They'd invade, and pretty soon the king's army would show up and chase them back into their wastelands, lickety-split. Not this time, though. Suddenly every move the Marauders make is brilliant. The king's army can hardly ever find them as they hide among the hills, preparing to strike again. And when they *do* find them, that grand army is battered and bruised every time."

The arm burrowed toward the collar again, and Rumpel-Stiltskin paused to give it a healthy swat. "Do ye know why that is, boy?" the gnome said, leering at Tom.

"Do ye know why everything goes right for the Marauders now?"

"Because . . . because of that monster with the horrible face?" answered Tom, shuddering anew at the memory.

"Pshaw," said Rumpel-Stiltskin, waving the hand he still had. "Not because of that beastie, not at all. It's because of their *luck*, boy. They've got hold of something that's giving them uncanny fortune. A charm, call it. And that's where *ye* come in. Ye're going to take that luck away." Rumpel-Stiltskin grinned, and tried to rub his hands together in a crafty gesture, but scowled when he remembered that there was no second hand to clasp.

Tom's head wobbled as he tried to comprehend it. "Take their luck away? How am I supposed to do that?"

Rumpel-Stiltskin held up his remaining hand and brought his thumb and forefinger together, until they were nearly touching. "Get *closer*," he said. "Closer to the heart of their army. Closer to this charm of theirs. That'll even the score."

"Are you mad?" Tom shook his head, realizing what a pointless question that was, and asked a better one. "Have you seen how many men they have? There must be a thousand!"

The gnome raised an eyebrow and shook his head. "Oh, far more than that, I suppose."

Tom folded his arms and cast a stern look at the little man. "Do you know what I think?"

Rumpel-Stiltskin considered the question. "Mostly stupid thoughts, I imagine," he said gravely.

Tom sniffed. "No! I think that maybe I shouldn't do anything you tell me. Because maybe you're up to no good."

Rumpel-Stiltskin put his hand on his chest, fingers splayed. His face contorted, as if he was attempting an innocent expression that did not come naturally. "*Me?* Up to no good?"

"Yes, you. You've been up to no good your whole life. I know you have."

The gnome puffed out his chest and tried to cross his arms, forgetting again that one of the limbs required for that pose was missing. He settled for planting his fist on his hip. "How *dare* ye! I've never done anything wrong, so far as ye know!"

Tom narrowed his eyes. "You tried to steal the queen's baby, for one."

The gnome's knees buckled, as if he'd been punched in the gut. "What do ye know about that?"

"Everything," Tom said. "The straw. The gold. The miller's daughter. *The baby.*"

"Ye don't know *anything* about that," Rumpel-Stiltskin said, jabbing a finger at Tom. "Nobody does!" He turned away and lowered his head. His shoulders bobbed up and down.

"I know. Lots of people know," Tom said. He took a step closer and listened intently because the gnome was still talking, but it was only a coarse whisper, soft as wind through the willow leaves.

"What does anybody know? I did everything for that girl . . . gave everything I had so that idjit king would spare her life . . . I tried to do good, but what good did it do me? Stupid, worthless Helena. She would have been *dead* without me! And how did she pay me back? By despising me. *Spurning* me. After all I did! Married a cruel king instead of me!"

Tom felt as if a noose was around his heart, squeezing it. He stepped closer and reached out to touch the gnome's shoulder and tell him he was sorry. Rumpel-Stiltskin suddenly whirled around with his eyes ablaze and his lips pulled back in a feral snarl. Tom pulled his hand back, afraid it might be bitten off.

Rumpel-Stiltskin roared. "I THOUGHT SHE'D COME *WITH* THE BLOODY BABY! THAT'S THE ONLY REASON I TRIED TO TAKE IT!"

Tom raised his hands and tried to think of something to say. The gnome lifted one leg and began shaking it in the air, and hopping around. Tom couldn't imagine why until the missing arm spilled out of the trouser leg and onto the ground. Rumpel-Stiltskin picked it up by the elbow and hugged it to his chest, quietly groaning with his eyes squeezed shut. The disembodied hand patted his cheek.

Tom watched for a while, growing queasier by the moment, and finally thought it would be best to change the subject. "Why do you want me to do this? You still haven't told me *why*."

Rumpel-Stiltskin's eyes slowly opened. For a moment, it seemed to Tom that the gnome's expression had softened. The icy stare had gone warm and watery, the bottom lip trembled, and a hint of color filled the gnome's wrinkled gray face. And then, just as quickly, the moment passed. A shadow fell over Rumpel-Stiltskin's countenance, the brow crashed down like the visor of a helmet, and the lips curled back to bare his broken teeth.

"Fine, ye stinking, rotten, treacherous child! Prying into my affairs and digging up my name! I'll tell ye why. I need to do *good*. I need to make *amends*. Is that reason enough for ye?" He choked out the words "good" and "amends" as if just speaking them aloud might make him vomit.

"Amends?" Tom said. "You mean . . . for all the bad things you've done?"

The gnome looked to the heavens and sighed, exasperated. "Do I have to explain every bloody thing? Isn't it obvious, ye fool? I have to balance the scales. Before it's too late."

"What do you mean, too late?"

Rumpel-Stiltskin shook his head. "Never ye mind about that," he grumbled. "But it has to be soon. Very soon."

Tom felt a chill creep from the nape of his neck to the tips of his toes. "But . . ." he said, hesitating. "This thing you want me to do . . . It's too hard. I'm afraid."

Rumpel-Stiltskin peered up at Tom with a cold, life-less look that froze Tom's bones. "*Ye're* afraid? *Ye* don't know what fear is, stupid boy. And ye won't till yer time is almost up. Do it, ye fool! Sneak up on the Marauders and see what happens. Then meet me back in the Dark Dell, and I'll keep my end of the bargain. I swear, I'll try to fix yer curse. When all this is done, ye *must go back to the Dark Dell!* Do ye remember the way?"

Tom brought his fingers to his lips and nibbled at the nails. "I remember the way. . . . But I just don't think I can . . ."

"*Try.* Tom, ye have to *try*," Rumpel-Stiltskin said, his hoarse voice cracking.

It was the first time the gnome had called him by name. Tom stood with his hands clutching the front of his shirt, unsure of what to say next.

The gnome's head tilted to one side. "Someone's com-ing," he said, lifting the disembodied arm. Absurdly, the hand on that arm pointed into the forest over Tom's shoulder.

Tom looked in that direction but saw nobody. He turned back, knowing that he'd been tricked again. And he was: The gnome was gone.

"Come back here," cried Tom, raising a fist. "I *hate* it when you do that! I'm not done asking you questions! That monster I just saw in Dram—it's the same kind as in the Dark Dell, isn't it?" He turned as he shouted, unsure which way the gnome had gone. "And the one in the Dark Dell *knows* you, doesn't she? Because she said something about somebody named Rum. And that's *you*, isn't it? It's 'Rum' for 'Rumpel-Stiltskin'! Explain that, will you? What's going on here? *Get back here!* I want to know what—"

Tom stopped when he found himself facing a pair of young men. *Not Marauders*, he swiftly concluded. But they were armed with swords dangling from their sides and bows already strung with arrows. As they got a good look at Tom, they lowered the bows so the arrows pointed to the ground.

One of the men was short and thick-chested, with curly brown hair. The other was tall and lean with a prominent nose and straight black hair to his shoulders. The tall one spoke first as his eyes scanned the trees around them.

"Uh . . . Who are you talking to, boy?"

Tom looked to the heavens. Despite their weapons, these two didn't seem like enemies. And after everything that had happened since he left his island home, he had no more patience for untruths. "I was talking to Rumpel-Stiltskin," he answered matter-of-factly.

"Rumpel-*who*-skin?" asked the short one.

Tom raised his hand chest-high. "A nasty little gnome. He's about this tall. Big pointy hat, fat belly, arms and legs like sticks. Oh, but one of his arms fell off and he's carrying it around like a piece of mutton, and *the hand is still moving, ha, HA, HA!*" Tom clapped both hands over his mouth and pressed down hard. He was close to breaking into hysterical laughter, and thought he might never be able to stop once he began.

The two men looked at each other. The tall one shrugged and the short one widened his eyes, nodded toward Tom, and twirled a finger near his temple.

"It's true," Tom said, unstopping his mouth. "I mean, about the gnome, not that I'm crazy. He vanished just before you got here. . . . He does that . . . sometimes . . ." The more he talked, the more he wished he'd kept his hand over his mouth.

The tall one peered at Tom, and he opened his mouth for a silent chuckle. "Rolf," he said, "you notice anything about this kid?"

"Besides . . . this?" Rolf replied, repeating the twirling-finger gesture.

"No. I mean, *look* at him," the tall one said.

Tom frowned back at the men, wondering what was going on.

Rolf looked at Tom with one eye narrowed, and then his eyebrows crept higher. "Oh. The hair, of course."

"Not just the hair," the tall one said. "The nose. The eyes. The freckles, even. Hey, Red, where you from?"

"Penwall," said Tom.

"And where're your folks?"

"I don't know," Tom said. "The Marauders came. My parents ran. I was . . . It's a long story."

"Bloody Marauders," said Rolf. "Locusts with swords, that's what they are!"

"Listen, Red, why don't you come with us? It's not safe here. . . . The Marauders might have scouts about. Besides, there's a friend of ours you ought to meet."

Tom nodded. He was hungry and thirsty, and they might have food and drink for him. Besides, he had a good feeling about these two. They were men of Londria who shared the same enemy: the Marauders. Still, there was something that had to be said. "I'll go with you. But you can't get close to me. And since you already think I'm crazy, I don't mind telling you why."

16

The two archers led the way with Tom twenty paces behind. Jordan and Rolf were agreeable men who humored him when Tom told them he was cursed and asked them to keep their distance. Since they'd come upon him shouting in the forest, they'd apparently drawn the conclusion that Tom was an eccentric but harmless child.

The two men didn't talk as they walked. They peered like wary birds into the woods around them, watching for enemies. Finally they passed another armed man who was standing guard. When Tom went by, the sentry's eyes widened and a hint of a smile flickered on his mouth. Tom tried to decipher the expression. It was almost as if the fellow recognized him.

Jordan turned, looking more relaxed now that they'd passed the sentry, and spoke to Tom. "Almost there. You know a man named Conrad, Red?"

"No, sir. My name is Tom, by the way."

"Right. Tom. Bet lots of folks call you Red."

"Not really," Tom said, thinking, *Not many folks ever talk to me at all.* "Who's Conrad?"

"Friend of ours," said Jordan.

"Good man," Rolf added.

"Good soldier," said Jordan.

They entered a grassy clearing in the forest, striped with the shadows of late afternoon. A camp with dozens of tents had been set up there. There were men milling around—as many as two hundred, Tom figured. Most carried swords by their sides, and many had bows in their hands and quivers on their backs. The bows were exceptionally tall, Tom noticed—nearly as tall as the men themselves. None of the men had armor that Tom could see, and there were only thirty horses or so among them.

"I can't go any closer," Tom said to Rolf and Jordan. They looked at each other, and Jordan rolled his eyes. Tom could tell they didn't really believe in his curse. And that was fine with him as long as they kept a safe distance from him.

"That's all right, Red," said Rolf. "*Tom*, I mean. We'll get Conrad and bring him here."

"Thank you, sir." Tom sat on the ground and crossed his legs, still wondering why he had to meet this Conrad. When Jordan and Rolf walked away, he peered into the forest behind him, looking high and low for the gnome. *When all this is done, ye must go back to the Dark Dell!* That's what Rumpel-Stiltskin had said. Almost as if he didn't expect to see Tom again until then. But why?

Tom heard footsteps approach from the camp, and

turned to see who it was. The man who strode toward him was about the same age as Jordan and Rolf. He was a more impressive figure, lean-waisted and broad-shouldered, with a sword hung by his side. Tom took a closer look at Conrad's face and grew more amazed with every detail he perceived.

Conrad had fiery red hair. Wide-set eyes of blue. Fair skin. A spattering of freckles across his cheeks. A small-ish nose that turned up at the end. In every way, every feature, he looked like the kind of man Tom hoped he'd grow up to be.

"Hello, young man. I hear I'm not supposed to get too close," Conrad said brightly, stopping many paces away. As Conrad stared down at Tom, his head listed slowly to one side and his mouth went slack. He brushed a hand across his hair. "Well," he said. "Now I see what they meant. You look like . . ." Conrad's voice withered, his brow furrowed, and a distant look came into his eyes. His attention drifted away, dwelling on something remote and profound. Then he shook his head, clearing it, and his gaze locked onto Tom.

"Who are you? Where'd you come from?" He fired words like darts.

Tom was startled. "Tom Holly . . . Penwall . . . but . . ."

"But *what*?" Conrad's eyes widened. "Never mind, how old are you?"

"Twelve . . . or so. Eleven, maybe."

Conrad leaned forward, gripping one fist inside the

other hand. "*Maybe?* What do you mean? Why don't you know?"

Tom looked down at his hands. They shook and his fingers felt numb. He looked up again into the face of this red-haired man he'd never seen until a minute before, and felt his heart swelling. "I don't exactly know because . . . my parents found me. When I was really young. I was abandoned, or lost, when the Marauders came. They took—"

"*Where* did they find you?" Conrad said fiercely. "*Where?*"

Tom wanted to run. The look in Conrad's eyes unnerved him. "It was . . . somewhere east of Penwall . . . closer to Toppingham . . . That's what my dad told me. . . ." He stopped because he wasn't sure Conrad was listening anymore. The red-haired man had dropped to his knees and covered his face with his hands. Behind him, Jordan and Rolf had been watching with smiles on their faces, nudging each other and whispering. Now they stood quietly, their glances flickering between the redheaded boy and the redheaded man.

Conrad uncovered his face and opened his eyes. He stared at Tom. "Twelve years ago, my wife and I were separated during an invasion. I fought while she fled with the rest of the town. I never saw her again. Many people from the town died that day. I was told she must have been among them."

Tom listened with his head moving in circles, nodding

yes and shaking no. It was dawning on him, what all this meant.

"She was heavy with child, Tom. A child I thought had never been born, to a wife I was sure I'd lost. But it must be you. You look just like me . . . except the parts that look like your mother. So my Lucena didn't die that day! She lived, at least long enough to"— Conrad gulped air and his jaw fell—"Wait. Tom! This woman who raised you, who said she found you, what does she look like?"

Tom put a hand to his throat, where it felt like a great lump had swelled up inside. "She . . . um . . . she's not very tall. Kind of short, really. And her hair is . . ." Tom stopped talking, because Conrad turned away and waved his hand.

"That's enough," Conrad said. "It's not Lucena. I thought for a moment . . . you know. That maybe she'd found someone else, and made up a story about finding you. But she wouldn't. Not my Lucena." Conrad drew a sleeve across the corner of his eye and took a deep breath. His face shifted as sadness, amazement, and joy bubbled to the surface in turn.

Tom recognized the emotions because he was feeling them too. For years he'd wondered what became of his birth parents. And now fate had steered him to his blood father. A new sensation came over him, one he couldn't remember experiencing before. *I feel lucky*, he thought. But his heart sank when he remembered

Gilbert and Joan Holly. Were they alive? Were they well? He wondered if that was the price he'd paid to meet this redheaded man: the loss of the good people who'd raised him. If that was so, it was too great a price by far, he decided, pressing his hands into his suddenly soured belly.

"So it's Tom, is it?" Conrad said, trying to smile. "That's a good name. Not the one we planned for you, though. You would have been Alexander. Or Alexandra, if you were a girl."

"Those are nice names," Tom said weakly.

Conrad pushed himself to his feet again. "What a day this is," he said, spreading his arms wide. "You're my boy. Imagine the stroke of fate that brought you here!"

Tom shook his head as Conrad beckoned. "I can't come closer. There's a curse. . . ."

Conrad was a pale man, but his face managed to go even whiter. "No," he said. "Don't say that. Don't tell me the curse is real!"

Jordan and Rolf gave each other a nervous glance and inched away from Tom.

Tom wasn't sure how many more surprises he could take. This time it felt like his heart crawled halfway up his throat. "You . . . you *know* about the curse?" he said.

Conrad lowered himself to the ground unsteadily and sat. He puffed his cheeks and whistled out a long gust of air. "My poor boy. You need to know what happened. Just before I lost your mother and you. It's a strange tale,

Tom. A very strange tale." He glanced over his shoulder and saw Jordan and Rolf still hovering nearby, listening with rapt interest. "And what do you two want? Oh, why not? Listen to my story, friends. But first fetch us something to drink and eat. This boy looks hungry." As the two men bustled away, Conrad pinched the bridge of his freckled nose. "It's my fault you have this curse, Tom. All my fault."

17

As Conrad told his story, Tom had his fill of bread and cheese and cider. The food tasted fine. But as the strange tale went on, Tom realized that the great secret of his life was about to be revealed, and it felt like rocks were tumbling in his churning gut.

"This is what happened about thirteen years ago," Conrad began. "My wife and I were in the forest near our home. Weeks before, when I was hunting in those woods, I'd found a beautiful waterfall that I wanted to show her. She was with child—with you, Tom—so I put her on our gentlest horse and led her into the forest.

"I knew the place well, but a sudden fog rolled in, and we were lost. I kept moving, sure I could find the way home, but I only plunged deeper into a part of the woods I'd never been before. And then we came upon a little clearing in the forest—like this one, but smaller. And strangely, the fog did not enter the clearing. It surrounded it, as if a wall of glass held it back. Even odder, there were two strange men in the middle of the clearing, sitting on either side of a tree stump. They were tiny folk—even smaller than a child like yourself, with enormous feet and hands, and gnarly faces, and dirty beards that just about brushed the ground when they sat."

When he heard this, Tom's head felt light, as if it might float off his shoulders. He decided not to interrupt the tale—his side of the story could wait—and he leaned forward to listen closely as Conrad went on.

"And on that tree stump between the little men was a chessboard. Chess, of all things—my favorite game in the world. The noblest game of all! Well, I went right up to them, meaning to ask if they could point me and my wife in the right direction. But they were so caught up in their game that they didn't notice me until I stood right beside them. Then they looked up at me, and it was easy to see who was winning. One of them had a face filled with fury while the other wore a grin like the crescent moon. 'Looky,' the happy one said. 'It's over for him!' And I did look. Now, you have to understand that chess is my passion. That match was nearly over—most of the pieces were gone from the table, and the grumpy fellow only had his king and a few pawns left. But I saw something in the game that neither of those two had noticed. And then I made my terrible mistake. My lovely wife knew I was going to do it, too. She knew me too well. Lucena said, 'Mind your tongue, Conrad.' But I couldn't resist the chance to show how clever I was. Call me a fool, but I piped up. I said to the fellow who was about to lose, 'Perhaps you should advance that pawn upon his king, my friend.' Well, the grump glared at me with tears in his eyes. But he took my advice. And the happy one took the bait! He gobbled up the pawn with his queen. And I clapped my hands and laughed. 'That's it, a stalemate for sure,' I cried. Do you know what a stalemate is, Tom?"

"No, sir."

"That's when any move a player makes puts his own king into check. In other words, the opponent could capture the king with the next move. But putting yourself into check is an illegal move, so you can't make it. It creates a deadlock, Tom. A tie. Nobody wins!" Conrad smiled ruefully. "I could never have imagined what happened next. It was as if those two little men had swapped faces, because the grump became joyous and the happy one was stoked with rage. Now, there was something leaning against the stump that I hadn't noticed before: a knobby staff made of some gleaming black wood, with the head of a horned creature carved on its top end. The fellow who would have won if I hadn't interfered grabbed that staff and waved it around furiously. 'Foul!' he screamed. 'Unfair! I'm the rightful winner! And ye,' he said, pointing the staff at me, 'ye should have shet yer mouth!'"

When he heard Conrad mimic that familiar, grating voice, Tom shuddered.

"Lucena reached down for my shoulder," Conrad went on. "'Let us go!' she said. Once again, I should have listened to her. I might have had a better, happier life, and we might still be together. But I've always been a stubborn man, Tom. I tried to reason with the little fellow. I told him, 'I'm sorry, good fellow, but it's only a game. You shouldn't let it bother you so.' But that only made him angrier.

"The little man screamed, 'Only a game? Ye fool, ye don't know what was at stake! But I'll show ye!' He pointed the black staff at Lucena, and the eyes on the carved face glowed orange. 'I curse yer unborn child!' he shouted. 'That child will grow up to bring misfortune to anyone it meets!' And then something roared out of that staff. I don't know how to describe it. Like a combination of light and wind. It struck my wife, here," Conrad said, mashing a fist into his stomach. "Knocked her right off the horse. I rushed over, and as I helped her up, I looked back at the two men. The one with the staff was staring at it with an expression of great surprise. 'Did ye see that?' he cried. 'It worked!' Well, the other fellow—the one I'd saved from defeat—dashed over and yanked the staff out of his opponent's hands. 'Oh no ye don't! It's a stalemate! That means I keep this another seven years! And as fer yer curse, I'm going to undo it, jest to rub yer stinking nose in it!' And then *he* pointed the staff at my wife, and called out, 'That child will bring nothing but *good* fortune to anyone it meets!' And out shot another bolt, right into my wife's belly again, and she hit the ground once more. I kneeled by her side to make sure she wasn't hurt, and those two villains raced into the woods, screaming and clawing at each other, fighting for the staff. I never saw—Hold on, Tom, are you feeling all right?"

Tom's face had gone pale, and he'd wrapped his arms around himself. He'd barely heard anything Conrad said after the part about the curse of misfortune. Conrad had to call his name again before he could answer.

So that's what happened to me, Tom thought. "Yes. I'm fine. Please, go on."

Conrad hesitated, peering closely at Tom before finishing the story. "A few months after that strange day, it was nearly time for you to be born. And then, as luck would have it, the Marauders came. Masses of them, sweeping down and burning villages and towns. I went to help fight them off. I left"—He took a deep breath—"I left Lucena behind, thinking she would be safe. But there was a second army of Marauders that we didn't know of. They snuck through a forest, where we couldn't see them, and attacked our town. When I returned from the battle, the town had been pillaged and ruined, and my house was burned to the ground. I was told everyone was slain as they ran away—even my poor wife, who was about to give birth. I searched for days, but never found her or anyone who knew what became of her." Conrad's voice had grown so soft Tom could barely hear it. "After that, I couldn't bear the sight of my own town. And so I left. For all these years, I've been helping patrol Londria's borders, spoiling for every battle I could find with the

Marauders. If only I'd stayed, I might have heard of you and your bad luck, Tom. I might have realized my child was alive."

Conrad dropped his head into his hands and rubbed his eyes with the tips of his fingers. Then his face popped up again, with a questioning look. "It doesn't make sense. Why is misfortune your curse? Why didn't the second spell work? It should have undone the first."

Tom squinted, concentrating. He'd been wondering the same thing. "I don't know," he said. "Maybe the second spell just *missed*, or something."

Conrad rapped his chin with his knuckles. "Or maybe you'll bring bad luck for a while—but then good luck after that?"

Wouldn't that be nice, Tom thought. "But do you remember the curse? Do you remember what they said?"

"I remember every word. It's just what I told you before. Yes, I recall that day perfectly. Which reminds me . . ." Conrad patted one of his pockets, slipped a hand inside, and pulled out a small white object.

"Catch, Tom," he said, and he tossed it. The thing bounced in the soft grass in front of Tom and rolled to a stop against his leg. He picked it up. It was a carved wooden game piece, shaped like a curving pillar, wide at the bottom and the top, where it ended in a crown.

"It's the king," Conrad said. "From that chess game in the woods. The little men left it behind. I've carried it with me ever since."

"For luck?" Tom asked.

"That's right. For luck." Conrad smiled at the joke. "Now I'm sure you have a story for me. Tell me what you know about those little men. That's right—I saw the look on your face when I described them. Tell me, Son. Tell me everything."

Tom twitched when he heard Conrad use that word: "son." It felt uneasy and out of place, although he had no doubt that this man was his true father. The image of Gilbert Holly flashed in his mind, smiling and waving from across the river at Tom's island home, a sack full of carved figures slung over his shoulder. No, the word didn't feel right to his ears. *Don't worry about that now,* Tom told himself, and he began his tale.

He spoke for an hour or more, starting with the first appearance of the gnome at his island home and finishing with the arrival of Jordan and Rolf. Conrad sat with his fingers clasped and his thumbs under his chin, closing his eyes to concentrate on the words, hardly moving. But Jordan and Rolf listened as raptly as children at a puppet show. They guffawed at the cantankerous antics of the gnome, wrinkled their noses in disgust when Tom stuck his hand into the coffin, shivered at the narrow escape from the quill-beast, clapped for the victory at Hazard, and whistled softly during the grisly demise of Toothless John. And when Tom told them about his final conversation with the gnome and the heartbreaking story of Rumpel-Stiltskin's love for Helena, they nodded and lowered their heads. Rolf blew his nose loudly into his sleeve.

"Prob'ly the only thing that wretched gnome ever loved," Rolf said through lips twisted by emotion.

"Probably," replied Tom. He looked at Conrad, who eased his eyes open now that the story was done.

"What do you think, sir?" Tom said.

"I think," Conrad said, "that my son is a remarkable boy. Brave and wise beyond his years. And I think I'd like to meet the man and woman who raised you, and shake their hands."

"I hope you can someday," Tom said quietly, wondering what that moment would be like. He stared down at his clasped hands. "I hope they're all right."

"We'll find them, Tom." Conrad said it with such conviction that Tom believed it was true. "Now, here is something else that I think," Conrad said. "I don't believe that gnome can be trusted."

"I was going to say the same thing," Rolf said.

Jordan put an elbow in Rolf's side, and whispered, "Hush, it's not your business!"

"Tom, who knows what that Rumpel-Stiltskin is up to?" Conrad said. "He's never done a decent thing in his life, as far as we know. It would be madness to do his bidding."

"He's right, Tom," Rolf said, shielding himself from Jordan's elbow. "He's a cheat and a crook, and a baby snatcher to boot. You know what he's really after? The spoils."

"Spoils?" Tom asked, lifting his head.

"Honestly, what do you know, Rolf?" grumbled Jordan.

"I know what a scoundrel is, that's what I know," Rolf snapped back. "It's obvious to me. Tom, that gnome wants you to cause the Marauders trouble, so he can sneak up and get his hands on all the riches they've plundered. The Marauders bring it with them, you know—stacked high on carts right in the middle of their army. The pile grows with every town they raid and burn."

Tom pondered that for a while. "I don't think that's what he wants. I think Rumpel-Stiltskin meant what he said. He's trying to make good after doing bad all his life."

"Make good by casting you into the mouth of danger?" Conrad asked. "That's a funny way to go about it. And why is he always disappearing on you, even when you need him?"

"I wondered about that too, sir," Tom said. "Until I saw the poster and the reward. He stays out of sight so he doesn't get caught, I guess."

"Hmph," Conrad said, frowning. "Tom, I know we just met, but I hope you'll listen to me like a father. I want you to stay away from the Marauders. Let us handle them."

Tom felt a jolt course through his limbs. "What do you mean? You're not going to attack them . . . are you?"

Conrad nodded. "Someone has to defend this land. Even if the king won't."

"The king," said Rolf, practically spitting the words. "Fine monarch he turned out to be. His army gets its nose bloodied a few times and he calls them back to surround his precious castle."

Jordan leaned close to his friend. "That big mouth of yours is going to get you into trouble one day, Rolf."

"It's true, though, Tom," Conrad said, shrugging. "The king is through trying to help us. Every general and every army he's thrown at the Marauders has limped home in disgrace. So we'll do this ourselves, drive these villains out of our land. But there's something strange about these Marauders, Tom. They've come before, but they were never the greatest soldiers. It's different now. Ever since this last invasion began, it seems they can't be defeated. I was with the king's army, until they ran home. I saw it happen. First we could hardly ever find the Marauders. Wherever we searched, they'd gone somewhere else. And when we *did* find them, every stroke of fortune went their way. One time, a fierce rain bogged us down while the sun shone on the enemy just a half mile away. Another time, their entire army fled across a bridge, and the bridge collapsed when we tried to follow. Once, we thought we had them and were creeping up at night, and a flock of honking geese gave us away. It's uncanny. I've watched a hundred arrows that we fired land harmlessly between their men! Time after time they elude us and evade us. And every time we miss, they disappear into the hills and valleys, and a day later another town or village is destroyed."

"Tell him about the rumors," Rolf said. Conrad shot him a displeased look.

"Rumors?" asked Tom.

Conrad sighed. "Lately, strange rumors have come to us. They say there's a new leader of these Marauders. He always stays at the heart of their army and never ventures to the front or the rear. The Marauders call him 'Big Boss.' We've never seen him, whoever it is. And something else, Tom. They say this Big Boss has a charm or talisman of some kind—something that brings them their uncanny luck. Whatever the charm is, it's large, because we've glimpsed something strange at the center of their army. Like an enormous litter, or a palanquin." Conrad saw Tom's quizzical expression, and explained. "A palanquin is a big box with long rods on either side, so it can be carried on the shoulders of servants. It's like a carriage without wheels. But there are no windows in this one, just solid walls, and only a small door on one side. We're not positive, mind you, but we think the charm is kept inside."

Conrad tugged at his chin for a while, thinking. The next thing he said took Tom by surprise.

"Do you know what I like about the game of chess, Tom?"

Tom shook his head.

"There's no luck in it, my boy. Not a bit. When you win at chess, you know it was because you were clever. Not because of a lucky roll of the dice or because you drew the right card at the right time. You were simply better." Conrad closed his eyes. "That's all I want from this battle. No more happenstance or strokes of luck. I don't even mind being outnumbered. Just let the better men win."

That's what I'm here for, Tom said inwardly. *To take their luck away.* But he had a feeling Conrad wouldn't like the idea.

"Well, their good fortune has to run out some time," Conrad said. He raised a hand and tightened it into a fist. "And it will happen tonight. We'll *make* it happen tonight. It's time for the endgame."

The red-haired man's expression was as cold and steely as the sword by his side, but Tom saw doubt haunt the eyes of Jordan and Rolf. He felt his stomach twisting inside him like a towel being wrung dry. "Sir," he began to say, but Conrad interrupted him.

"Will you do me a great favor, Tom? Will you call me 'Father'? I'd like that very much."

"All right . . . ," Tom replied. He almost said it right then, but the word wouldn't come out easily. In a strange way, calling this man "father" would feel like a betrayal of Gilbert Holly, the only father he'd ever known. "But if you're really going to attack the Marauders, then you should let me go and sneak into the middle of their army. If it's true, what you said about their charm, you need me to do this."

Jordan and Rolf's expressions brightened at these

words, but Conrad's grew dark. He stood up and crossed his arms. "No, Tom. *No!* I just found you. Do you think I'd let you walk into that pack of butchers and thieves?"

Tom stood up and folded his arms as well. "And I just found you. Do you think I'd let you attack an army that can't be defeated?"

They stood facing each other, a man and his miniature reflection. Rolf chuckled. "Face it, Conrad. He's just as pigheaded as you!"

A black-bearded man called out to Conrad from behind them. Conrad gave Tom a final stern look and a disapproving grunt, and turned to see what was the matter. The man waved Conrad over.

"Wait here, Tom," Conrad said. "I'll be back, and we'll settle this."

Tom nodded. Conrad walked toward the camp where a group of men waited to speak to him. Jordan and Rolf went with him. As Tom watched, he noticed that the other men, dozens of them, gathered around Conrad and listened raptly, nodding every now and then. *He's a leader,* Tom thought, feeling a surge of pride.

While he waited, Tom opened his pack. He frowned at the heavy pile of coins inside. They were slowing him down, and he didn't need so much, so he scooped most of them out and left them in a pile. He'd ask Conrad to hold them for him.

He checked on the glow-toad, who seemed perfectly comfortable at the bottom of the jar, sitting in the nest of grass that Tom had added. It gobbled a pair of fat grasshoppers that Tom dropped inside, then closed its eyes and dozed. Tom covered the jar again and stuffed it into the pack.

A twig broke in the dense forest behind him. Tom turned and peered into the shadows. There was motion, deep in the trees. Between the clusters of leaves, he saw something that looked like the hide of a sheep. *But there's no sheep in a forest.*

Tom's mind leaped back to what he'd seen shortly after he left the Dark Dell: Marauders, clad in the skin of rams. He shuddered. He looked back at the camp, but Conrad was still talking to the men. *I'd better make sure,* he thought.

He started walking, and then, spurred by a growing fear, he broke into a run. Soon he saw the men in front of him. Two Marauders. They loped through the woods at a pace that was fast, but not so fast that they might make too much noise. Somehow they'd slipped through a gap in the sentries that surrounded the camp.

Tom wondered if the Marauders had seen Conrad's army. *Of course they did! They're spies! And now they'll tell the others.* Conrad's men were already outnumbered, and now their sole advantage—surprise—was going to vanish like the gnome. Tom felt a fierce pang in his gut because it occurred to him that this might be his fault. *Did I bring the bad luck with me? Did those spies find the camp because of my curse?*

There were two things he could do, he realized. He could turn back and warn the others. *Or I can try to stop them myself.* He started running faster, not caring how much noise he made.

Tom began to close the gap between himself and the spies. He thought he saw one of them glance back over his shoulder, but wasn't sure that the man had seen him. The spies darted into a thick cluster of trees that was heavy with underbrush, out of sight for a moment. Tom followed, and when he emerged from the thick bushes, he didn't see anyone ahead of him anymore. From the side, a foot darted out from a tree and caught him on the shin. Tom stumbled and lost his balance, rolling over roots and rocks before coming to a stop, his teeth clenched tight and his hands grasping his lower leg that was afire with pain.

He looked up to see the spies approaching. They were young, powerful men with beards plucked clean in the middle of their chins, and mustaches hanging like tusks on the sides of their mouths. They had the tribe's usual scars down the sides of their faces. Tom felt his throat cinch up tightly when he saw that many of the little scars were freshly carved and raw. There was a whisper of steel as the spies drew short, wide swords from the scabbards at their sides.

"If there's one thing a spy hates, it's being spied on," said one of the Marauders, picking at one of the scabs on his cheek. "And now that we've seen your little army, we need to make sure the army doesn't know it's been seen."

"Don't come near me," Tom said. "I'm warning you!"

The Marauders laughed and raised their swords. "Tell you what, boy," the taller one said, stepping closer. "If you don't scream, we'll make it quick."

Between Tom and the murderous pair, a creature blundered out of the bushes, bounding clumsily on all fours. It was a small pudgy thing with dark brown fur, a lighter muzzle, rounded ears, and a nub of a tail. *Bear cub*, Tom thought.

The cub waddled toward the Marauders. "Get out, stupid beast!" snarled the taller one. He drew back his leg and delivered a savage kick. The cub squealed as it tumbled through the air and crashed into the underbrush. The Marauders chuckled and turned their attention back to Tom.

Tom felt the sensation again—something fluttering inside his head. There was a thunderous growl from the underbrush that made the heads of the Marauders spin back toward the noise. The bushes thrashed and shook, and something many times larger than the cub, larger even than the men, broke out into the open.

The mother bear roared, and rose up on her hind legs as she bore down upon the taller Marauder. The Marauder swung his sword, but the bear swatted it away with a powerful paw, bending the man's wrist back with an awful snap. He turned to run, but the bear was already on him, engulfing him with long black claws and a savage, gaping mouth. There was a shrill, terrible scream, then a muffled cry, and then only sounds that made Tom want to cover his ears.

The other Marauder didn't consider saving his companion. By the time it occurred to Tom to look up, the second spy was running pell-mell into the woods at a pace Tom knew he could never match.

Tom turned, averting his eyes from the terrible sight of the bear and her victim, and headed back for the camp. He saw the Marauder's sword on the ground, picked it up, and brought it with him.

Conrad groaned. "They were spies for the Marauders? Are you sure, Tom?"

Tom nodded, and held up the discarded sword with two hands. Conrad smacked his forehead with his fist. Then he turned and shouted to the men behind him. "Jordan! Rolf! Spread the word: We've been seen. Tell the rest, we need to move quickly."

As Jordan and Rolf ran to alert the camp, Tom rose up on his toes, feeling light with relief. "So you won't attack after all?"

"We most certainly will, Son. But first we'll make it look like we're retreating. Then I'll take a few men and get close, where I can signal the others to attack. This is our chance, Tom. We've been waiting for them to come to Dram. We lured them here. We've been spreading rumors about hidden riches in Dram, hoping those greedy devils would rise to the bait. And it worked. They haven't even burned the town yet, as they usually do. They're busy tearing down the buildings, searching for gold. We have to strike them tonight, before they vanish into the hills again."

"But if the king's army couldn't beat them, how can you?" Tom knew he was whining, but couldn't help it.

"Tom, they're so close to the forest that we can sneak up without them seeing. We have longbows that can reach the peak of that hill, even from the edge of the forest. We *will* beat them, Son. Or at least we'll punish them greatly for what they've done. You'll see."

"And what about the quill-beast? Have you ever seen its face, Fath—um, sir?"

Conrad winced, understanding what Tom had been about to say and chosen not to. Then he shook his head and spoke quietly. "No. I haven't seen its face." He turned to look at the camp behind him, where the men had begun to strike down the tents and gather up the weapons. "We'll deal with the monster, Tom. And the Marauders. Just promise me you'll stay out of the way."

Tom looked into the trees and up at the sky. "I'm sorry,

sir, I can't make that promise. I think it's my fault the spies found you. My bad luck made that happen. And I'm making it worse, every minute I stay here. If you mean to attack them, then you need me to do this. Otherwise you'll fail, because of this charm they have."

Conrad straightened his back and put his hands on his hips, and suddenly seemed to have grown much taller. He thrust out his jaw and cast a stern look at Tom. "You will not go anywhere near them. I'm ordering you! Don't make me put you in chains!"

Tom could feel Conrad's will pressing down on him. He widened his stance, to better bear its weight, and did the best he could to meet that fierce gaze. He shook his head and pointed over his shoulder with his thumb. "The last man who came near me got killed by a bear. The one before that got cooked by lightning. I'm sorry, sir. But you can't stop me. And you *shouldn't* stop me. I'm the best weapon you have. Better than your swords and longbows." He lifted his pack and slipped his arms through the straps.

"Tom . . ." sputtered Conrad.

"I'm glad we found each other, sir," Tom said, shrugging the pack into place. "I hope we can find each other again. Please don't follow me. . . . It isn't safe." He turned and walked into the woods as Conrad bellowed for him to come back.

19

T om stayed hidden at the edge of the forest, waiting for darkness to come. The weary sun tucked itself behind the western hills, and the stars ignited one by one.

To his left was the town of Dram. It was just beginning to burn. The Marauders had gone through every building, piled the valuables into carts in the middle of the road, and driven them away. Their horsemen galloped down the street and threw their torches onto the roofs of the shops and taverns, shouting and laughing as if it were a holiday. Columns of black smoke rose up to support the dusky sky.

A wide, gently sloping hill was before him. It was a farm or pasture, or both, judging from the rock walls and wooden fences that lined the hill, and the domes of hay that dotted the slope. But now it was infested by the army of the Marauders, a thousand strong or more. Packs of them came down to the base of the hill and lit roaring fires, feeding the flames with broken pieces of the fences, surrounding the army with a dotted chain of orange light.

Tom saw other shapes on the hill in the failing light. Near the top was a row of wagons, piled high and covered with cloth. *All the treasure they've plundered*, Tom thought. He wondered which one held the wealth of Penwall. And did anything in those piles belong to Gilbert or Joan Holly? He ground his teeth and curled his fingers, clawing into the earth and seizing a fistful of dirt and leaves.

He saw something else, at the very top of the hill. A rectangular box, not as big as the wagons. He remembered the name that Conrad had used for it: the palanquin. *That's where it is*, he thought. *The source of their luck is in the palanquin. That's where I have to go.*

The sky dimmed to an inky blue. It was dark enough now; Tom knew it was. But still he waited, gnawing at his fingernails, wondering how he could possibly get past those fires and all the way up that hill. The curse had kept him safe from small groups of attackers before, but how could it ever protect him if an alarm went up and a thousand men wanted him dead?

On the other side of the Marauders' army, the endless hills of Londria rolled on like ocean waves. The curved edge of something bright and silver white appeared on the horizon. *The moon*, Tom thought, squeezing his eyes shut. When it rose, it would cast its pale light over the world, and creeping up the hill undetected would be even harder. Another problem! He was suddenly weary. His arms and legs went as soft and heavy as wet clay.

Since he'd left his island, hope had been a slippery, squirmy thing, trying always to slip out of his grasp. As he looked at the hill and the obstacles that surrounded its crest, he thought he might lose that grip for good.

It has to be now, he told himself. *If I don't do this now, I may be cursed forever. And Conrad might die. Along with Jordan and Rolf and a lot of others.* He bowed his head and allowed himself to picture a life without the curse. He imagined finding his mother and father, and running to them. He would laugh and shout to them, and tell them that the curse was gone. They would be amazed; their eyes would be huge, and they would cry with joy. And he would leap into their arms for a wonderful, crushing embrace.

Tom raised his head and opened his mouth for a long, deep breath of air. And then, trying to ignore the fact that he was probably rushing headfirst into his own doom, he pushed himself to his feet and ran, hunching low, out of the woods.

Take away their luck, and let the better men win.

There was a streambed in front of him, and he slid down the bank where he could stay hidden from wary eyes. He followed the burbling stream as it angled toward the hill, and then poked his head up to survey the scene. There was a fire to either side, and he saw the dark silhouettes of Marauders pacing around the burning heaps of wood. The fire to the right was closer, but there was a low stone wall between those men and Tom that might conceal him. He climbed over the bank of the stream and crawled, using his elbows and knees to wriggle toward the wall, hoping the tall grass was enough to keep him hidden. To his ears the rustle of grass was deafening.

He reached the stone wall and stayed there for a moment, panting. The black shadow of the wall trembled as the flames rose and fell. Orange light poured through a gap between two stones nearby, and he crawled toward that spot, meaning to peer at the men on the other side. When he rested his hand on one of the stones, it shifted and settled, and the stone that was perched above it rolled off, landing on the other side with a thump.

"What was that?" asked a voice near the fire. Tom gulped. He put his eye to the hole in the wall and saw one of the Marauders facing his way, looking at the fallen stone.

"What was *what?*" asked another.

"Something over there," said the first. He leaned forward with his hands on his knees, and squinted.

"Just a critter, you milksop," said the other.

"Don't be so sure," said the first. He put a finger to his lips, signaling for the others to be quiet.

Tom stopped breathing. His body stiffened. He watched the Marauder reach down, grab the hilt of his sword, and draw it from the scabbard in a smooth and soundless motion. The blade flashed with the orange light of the fire.

The fire popped and crackled, and a hot ember was ejected high into the air. It soared up in a graceful arc, paused at the apex, and fell again in a smooth curve that ended down the back of the approaching Marauder's shirt. He shrieked and dropped the sword, and bent his arms back in wild contortions, clawing at the ember that worked all the way down to his waist. The rest of the Marauders around the fire, twelve or more, roared with laughter. Tom didn't wait to see what would happen next. He crawled away, faster now that he didn't think he would be heard, staying near the wall where the shadows cloaked him.

He went up the hill on all fours, collecting scrapes and bruises. There was a broad, unoccupied space between the ring of fire at the bottom of the slope and the main army encamped on the top, and so he was able to make swift progress once he'd left the sentries behind. When he was halfway up, he heard a commotion on the other side of the hill. He peeked over the wall, wondering if the attack was already launched before he could get close to the palanquin.

It didn't look like an attack, though. Near one of the distant fires at the bottom of the hill, he saw men moving about. There was one man who had his arms bound behind him, surrounded by others with swords. Tom squinted, trying to see better, but they were just tiny shadow puppets at this distance. *A prisoner?* he wondered, ducking out of sight again. If a prisoner was taken, perhaps that meant that Conrad's men were getting close.

Tom scrambled forward, feeling a new sense of urgency. Before long, he found himself with a fresh problem: He'd reached the end of the stone wall. He looked anxiously at the moon, nearly full, which had vaulted clear of the horizon. The sky elsewhere was clear, with stars bobbing in a sea of ink. There would be no clouds to cloak the moon's dangerous light.

There were humped stacks of hay in front of him, scattered across the hillside. All he could do, he figured, was run from one to the next, and hope that not one of the thousand pairs of eyes noticed a small boy coming toward them. "This is impossible," he whispered to himself. *Am I even doing the right thing?* He considered the alternatives. *Should I go up now, before it gets even brighter? Should I wait until the attack begins and there's some confusion? Or am I already close enough to make a difference?* The trouble was, even though he'd lived with the curse all his life, he still couldn't predict the exact effect it would have.

Tom closed his eyes and clenched his fists, concentrating. "Rumpel-Stiltskin," he whispered. "I need help. This was your idea. Why aren't you here to tell me what to do? I can't do this alone. I can't! Please, come here!" He waited, and felt a rush of cold air pass over him. His eyes flew open, and he whirled around, looking eagerly in every direction. Nothing would have made him happier at that moment than to hear that gruff voice spew some terrible insult. But the gnome wasn't there.

Time was running out; he could sense it in the tightness of his chest. And there was another feeling within, harder to describe, like a whisper coming from his heart. His gaze was drawn to the top of the hill where the wagons were piled high with plunder. And there, near the wagons, sat the palanquin. *What's in there?* he asked himself. *The reason you're here,* that inner voice replied. His flesh erupted in tiny, shivering goose bumps as a fresh thought came to him. He couldn't believe he didn't think of sooner.

Maybe I can take it, whatever it is, he thought. *And bring it with me wherever I go. Because if its good luck is as strong as my bad luck . . . I'll be ordinary.* The idea was so perfect, so wonderful, that he hardly dared to believe it was possible. And the best part was he wouldn't have to depend on the shifty gnome for a cure.

He wondered what the charm was. An amulet? A ring? A wizard's staff, like the one that caused all his woes? Was it a physical object at all, like the useless stuff that filled the trunk in his home on the island? Whatever it was, if he could get to it and he could carry it, it was coming with him.

With that beautiful but delicate possibility embraced in his heart, he got to his feet and ran.

There was a haystack less than one hundred strides

away—still a hard run since he was going uphill. With every step he grew more certain that somebody would call out from the camp above or the outposts below. He finally reached the stack, ran to the side in the shadow of the moonlight, and pressed his back against the warm, scratchy straw. His chest heaved, and he felt sweat biting at the scrapes on his knees.

Tom peered around to see if anyone was approaching. In the distance it looked as if the prisoner was being marched up the hill. A hood had been pulled over his head, and one of the Marauders led him while several more walked behind with swords at the poor fellow's back. The prisoner stumbled and fell. The swordsmen laughed.

Tom scowled. There wasn't much he could do for that poor soul. But maybe Conrad's attack would come in time. And for the attack to succeed, he had to get to the charm.

Another hundred strides away, he saw the dark bell shape of the nearest haystack. It was smaller than the others, but still a place to hide and rest for a moment. He took a few deep breaths and bolted toward it.

When he was halfway there, the dark, humped shape began to move. It rose, not a haystack at all, but some enormous creature that towered over him, twice as tall as a man.

"I can see in the dark," the creature said, growling and clicking and hissing the words. Tom knew the voice. It was the quill-beast—the monster with the face nobody could bear to see. He wailed and fell to the ground, where he curled up with his back to the thing and covered his head with his hands.

20

Tom felt the *whump, whump* of heavy footsteps reverberating through the ground. The pounding stopped, and he heard the deep, whistling breath of the quill-beast, and the scrape of its feet in the soil. Tom wondered if his curse could possibly save him now—or if this creature would even be affected. Animals were not; only people. Which was this?

"What do you think you're doing?" the quill-beast said in that strange three-part voice.

"N-n-nothing," Tom stammered. "J-j-just looking around." He had his thumbs pressed hard against his eyelids, and his head tucked between his trembling shoulders.

"Looking around." The quill-beast hissed down at Tom. "Run away, little boy. Run away, or die."

I've failed, Tom thought. *I'm not going to make it.* And yet this was the second time the quill-beast had him at his mercy, but hadn't killed him. "Please," Tom whimpered. "Let me go past you. I don't mean you any harm."

"Go past me? Are you mad?" The quill-beast snorted. "Let me see your face," he said.

"No . . . please," Tom whimpered. "I'm afraid."

"Show your face," the quill-beast said, loud and stern. He followed it with a low, rolling growl.

Tom took his arms off his head and turned toward the monster.

"You can open your eyes," the quill-beast said. "My face is cloaked."

Tom eased his eyelids open but kept his gaze down. He saw the thing's legs and bare feet sticking out from the bottom of the cloak. The limbs were entirely covered in quills, every one ending in a wicked point. Tom's eyes slowly moved up. Even in the pale moonlight, he could see that the cloak was in shreds. He saw leathery hands with more fine quills on their backs, and lethal claws on the tip of every finger. One of the hands rose, and a finger pointed at Tom.

"You again? You were in that village. In the street," the beast said.

Tom risked a look at the creature's face. The cloak had a hood that was drawn up, but he still caught a glimpse of the grotesque features inside. His stomach lurched, and cold terror flowed through his veins. He howled and covered his eyes with a forearm. "Please . . . don't kill me," Tom pleaded.

An angry rumble came from the throat of the beast. "I could shred you with a touch of these hands. Or frighten you to death with this face. But I don't kill. My task is to scare men away. Look at you, though—the boy who stays and talks when grown men cry and run! Tell me, why do you want to fly into the hornet's nest? What brings you here?"

A voice called down from the hilltop. "Hey! Beastie! Who you talking to down there? You catch someone?"

The beast whirled toward the voice, away from Tom. "Leave me be, you fool! I'll tell you if I need you!" He reached up and tugged his hood back to offer a glimpse of his face in the moonlight.

"Aaagh! Never mind!" screeched the voice at the top of the hill. The quill-beast chuckled. He pulled the hood across his face again and turned back toward Tom.

Tom tried to control the panic that coursed through his mind. He knew his curse wouldn't save him. If anything was going to happen to the quill-beast, it would have begun by now. But perhaps he wouldn't need the curse after all. Something important was rising up from the depths of his memory, trying to make itself known, if Tom could only control his fear enough to think clearly.

"You . . . you don't like the Marauders, do you?" Tom asked, buying time.

The quill-beast hissed and spat. "Vile, soulless, greedy swine."

Tom clasped his shaking hands together, summoning his courage. "You . . . you just . . . scare people away. Make it easier for them to invade."

There was an angry growl that made Tom cringe.

"Don't judge me, child. I have my reasons," the terrible voice said.

The fear surged again. The urge to run was almost undeniable. Tom's legs pawed at the ground, trying to get away by themselves. Tom pounded his fist on his wounded knee, hoping the sharp pain would clear his senses. He was sure there was something important to remember. And it had something to do with . . .

"The Dark . . . Dell," he said through gritted teeth.

"*What?*" spat the quill-beast. "*What* did you say?"

"The Dark Dell," Tom repeated as his thoughts sputtered. "There's . . . another . . ."

"What do you mean?"

Tom heard the rustling of the cloak, and the voice was louder, almost directly over his head. *He's leaning over me,* he thought, staring at the ground and shaking harder than ever.

"I mean," he said, so frightened that he was huffing between words, "there's . . . another one . . . of you . . . in the dell. . . ."

"You've been there?" cried the monster. "Did you see her, the one like me? Was she alive? Was she well?" Tom heard the bristling of quills and a thump in the grass as the beast dropped to his knees, right next to Tom. Then he had to bite off a scream as he felt a blinding pain in his thigh. One of the quills had stuck out through the cloak, and its tip struck Tom.

The beast grunted and shuffled back, taking the quill

out with it. Tom clapped a hand over the spot and fought back tears.

"I hurt you." The beast groaned. His head, still covered by the hood, slumped forward. He raised his leather-palmed hands. The wicked talons flashed in the moonlight. "Do you see? Do you see this skin I wear? Child, the one you saw in the Dark Dell is Maud, the one I love. But for us to hold each other brings pain . . . for us to look at each other brings terror. But still, I need to know that Maud is well. That the antidote is working."

That's it, Tom thought. His mind cleared, and the secret conversation he'd overheard between the two Marauders at the mouth of the Dark Dell came back to him. "There is no antidote!" he said.

The cloaked head tilted up again. "What do you mean, child?"

"There's no antidote because there was never a poison," Tom said, averting his eyes.

The clawed hand reached out as if the monster wanted to seize Tom's arm, but it stopped short. "How can you know this? I don't believe you!"

Tom concentrated, remembering another secret he'd overheard. "Water, wine, and mustard-seed. That's all there is in the antidote."

The quill-beast gasped. "Maud said . . . it *reeked* of mustard."

Tom sat up. "I overheard two of them on their way to the Dark Dell. One was named Melch."

"Melch!" raged the beast, raking the air with his claws. "He was the one that came and told me what they'd done!"

"They tricked you, didn't they?"

The cloaked head nodded. "Melch said they poisoned her and would let her die if I didn't do their leader's bidding for one year." The quill-beast began to breathe faster, snorting like a bull. The breath came out of the shadows of the hood in puffs of steam. On the arms and legs, the quills quivered and bristled. Tom sensed fury building.

"Do you know who their leader is? Big Boss?" Tom asked.

"I do not," the quill-beast said, rising to his feet and flexing his talons. He stared at the hilltop. "They don't let me near their precious Big Boss. And he stays hidden most of the time. But Melch has returned. I have *seen* Melch." The monster growled again, and the growl built to a roar.

"Wait," Tom said. "I helped you, didn't I? I wonder if you could—"

"I am *done* with this!" shouted the quill-beast. Tom knew that heads everywhere must be turning his way, and everyone would know that there was an intruder. He heard shouts from all around.

"I must go to her now," the beast cried. "Maud's heart was broken when I left, and I don't know how long she can bear the pain. I am leaving. But first . . .

Melch!" The beast headed straight up the hill, leaving Tom alone in plain sight. He looked down and saw men streaming up toward him, pointing and stringing arrows in their bows.

21

Tom watched the quill-beast stride up the slope, picking up speed. Even from this distance he could hear the screech of his quills rubbing against one another. The Marauders sensed that something was wrong and fumbled for their weapons. Tom saw the clawed hands of the beast reach up and push back the hood—thankfully he could not see the nightmarish face from behind—and the men on the hilltop quailed and ran or threw themselves on the ground and covered their faces.

Tom watched with his hands clasped on top of his head, desperately trying to think. He suddenly realized the opportunity that lay before him. With the beast on a rampage, he might be able to follow behind and make it to the palanquin unnoticed. He ran up the hill, keeping his gaze on the trampled grass in the wake of the monster. Ahead of him the quill-beast roared and the men wailed. A single arrow whisked over Tom's head and landed in front of him, but when he turned around, he saw that the Marauders below had broken off their pursuit, unwilling to risk a glimpse at the ghastly face of the monster.

Tom's legs ached from running uphill, and his strides grew short. The sting in his knees was joined by the burning of the tiny hole the quill had made in his thigh. But he forced his legs to rise over and over again, trying to stay close behind the raging beast who took the crest of the hill and swept his face right and left to terrorize those who might resist him. All the while he howled the name of his prey: "*Meeeelch!*"

Tom reached the flattened top of the hill a moment later. The army was in chaos as the beast stalked among them. It seemed to Tom that half were in a blind hysteria, and half tried to maintain order. Some ran pell-mell down the hill, tripping and tumbling in their panic. Others tried to untie the horses and ride away while the keepers of the horses battled to prevent their escape and ruthlessly cut their own men down. Tom saw men shoot arrows at the beast with their eyes closed, and, of course, miss badly. A Marauder limped past Tom, screeching, with an arrow lodged in his thigh. Men collided, cracking their heads together and falling in a stupor.

The tableau was so insane that Tom forgot his plan for a moment. And then his gaze landed on the palanquin at the very center of the hilltop. He ran toward it, undetected amid the bedlam.

The palanquin was just as Conrad described it—a rectangular box, ten feet long and six feet tall, with sturdy poles sticking out from the front and back so it could be carried by a team of men. It rested on stubby legs a few feet off the ground, creating a dark, inviting hiding space below. Tom rolled underneath to get out of sight for the moment.

He felt something moving under his shirt, like tiny legs pawing at his throat. *The All-key*, he thought. He pressed his palm against the spot, and felt the little piece of metal twisting and bending, growing shorter and longer and shorter again, as if it could not settle on a single shape.

There was a terrible scream amid all the other sounds. Tom peered out from the dark space and looked for the quill-beast, holding up his hand at an angle that would shield him from the frightful face. The monster stood with his back to Tom, looming over a man who cowered on the ground. It was Melch, the one Tom saw outside the Dark Dell whispering the secret of the antidote. So it was true, after all: Speaking that secret aloud was the most unfortunate thing the old Marauder could have done that day, and only the consequences had been delayed. The quill-beast reached down with a spiny paw and plucked up the screaming Marauder by the neck. Tom turned away, not wanting to see, but he heard the scream come to an abrupt end. When he turned back, Melch was lying in a heap on the ground, as limp and motionless as a wet rag. The quill-beast headed over the hill, howling the name of his beloved Maud.

Tom knew his time to act was running out. Soon the pandemonium would settle down, men would recover their wits and uncover their faces, and they might spot the intruder among them. He pulled out the key from his shirt and drew the leather strap over his head. The dangling key still oozed from one form to another, holding one shape for only a second, and then changing anew.

He crawled out from under the palanquin and stood in front of the door, raising the key. Then he saw why it was in constant transformation: There were three different locks on the door, one above the other. *Must be something awfully important inside,* he thought. He peered over his shoulder to see if anyone was watching. A few Marauders were shouting, trying to restore order. Many were still on the ground, hiding their faces, and were just now daring to look around.

Hurry, Tom, he scolded himself. He brought the key to the first lock, and it quickly resolved itself into a short, fat shape with a single peg at the end. He slid it into the keyhole, turned it, and heard something inside slide and click.

The key again changed, flowing like honey, when he brought it to the second hole. This time it assumed a longer, wider form with three notches. Again the lock turned easily.

For the third lock, the key grew longer and wider still, with fanglike projections at the end. The last lock turned, and Tom pulled on the door knob, hoping the hinges didn't squeak. It glided open in silence. Once the gap was wide enough, he took a final look behind him.

Nobody was looking his way yet. He stepped inside and eased the door shut, and slipped the strap that held the key over his head.

Tom took a moment to slow his breath and calm his mind. His heart thumped so hard and fast that he could hear it inside his ears.

I made it, he thought. He was happy that his presence might take away the advantage the Marauders had enjoyed during this long rampage and give Conrad's men a fair, fighting chance. But there was something he wanted to do for himself as well. He wanted to see if he could find, in this lightless box, the permanent cure for his curse: a charm that he could carry away. *I'll bring it to Conrad first,* he thought, and his heart warmed at the idea. *He can use it to beat the Marauders, and then give it back to me. I can be part of the world again. I can live a normal life, like any other boy.*

It was time to see what lay inside. His hands shook as he took off his pack and reached for the jar that held the glow-toad. It occurred to him that the poor creature might have been killed or injured with all the running he'd been doing. But when he pulled the cork from the jar, he saw the welcome yellow glow. The fat amphibian blinked up at him with round, watery eyes, and Tom was certain it looked annoyed. It even opened its mouth and showed him its tongue. But the toad also seemed to sense that its light was needed, and the dim glow became brighter.

This is it, Tom thought. He looked around, searching for the charm, whatever it might be. But what he saw was not what he expected.

The inside of the palanquin was spare. There was a small table and a single stool beside it. A tray on the table had on it a few scraps of food, a metal pitcher, and an iron cup. There was a candle on the table with a thin stream of smoke still flowing from the wick. As Tom stared, the smoke died.

Tom swallowed hard. Near his feet there was a heavy iron ball with a chain attached to it. The chain snaked across the floor and disappeared under what he'd first thought was the far wall but now realized was a thick curtain that spanned the width of the interior. From what his memory told him about the outside of the palanquin, he thought there might be three more feet of space on the other side of that cloth.

He took two hesitant, trembling steps and was there. The jar with the glow-toad was cradled in one arm. He reached out and pushed the curtain slowly aside with the other hand.

There was a narrow bed on the other side. A girl sat on it, curled up in one corner, staring at him with enormous, frightened eyes. One of her arms was wrapped around her knees, hugging them to her chest. She had the knuckles of the other hand clamped between her teeth.

Tom stared at her and she stared back. The longer

Tom looked, the more his jaw sagged. Numbness swept from the top of his head to the tips of his fingers. The jar slipped from his grip and smashed on the floor.

The girl took her hand away from her mouth, revealing her entire face. Her look of fear became a look of wonder. She sat up so that she was resting on her knees. Tom gawked.

She had wide-set eyes of blue. A small nose that turned up at the end. A spattering of freckles across her cheeks. And the brightest red hair he'd ever seen, apart from his own and Conrad's.

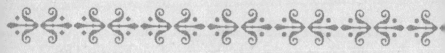

CHAPTER

22

The redheaded girl glanced at the glow-toad, which had landed upside down on the shattered pieces of the jar. The toad finally managed to flop onto its belly, and then hopped away and settled its fat bulk down in a clear spot on the floor with its throat puffing in and out, and an indignant look on its warty face.

Her gaze came back to Tom, and she smiled. "It's you," she whispered. "It's you, isn't it?"

Tom's thoughts were a blur. He tried three times to respond before words came out, as soft and meek as mice. "What . . . what do you mean?" But the truth was dawning on him. And he wondered why it hadn't occurred to him before. It explained everything.

"You're the other one," she said. "You're my brother. Born the same day as me." A tear tumbled down her cheek. "I can't believe you're here," she said, although her mouth was twisted with emotion and the words were hard to understand. She crawled to the edge of the bed and opened her arms, and Tom hugged her, squeezing as hard as he dared as she sniffed against his shoulder. He closed his eyes and smiled wide, trying to remember the last time someone had dared to touch him, even the good people who raised him.

"Wait," he said, pushing her away. "I can't be sure it's safe . . . to be close to you. . . ."

"It's all right," she said, seizing his hands. "I've thought about this my whole life. I'll be safe from your curse. I *know* I will!"

Tom held her by the shoulders. "You know about the curse?"

"Of course," she said. "But you don't know what happened, do you?"

Tom thought back to the story Conrad had told him, about the little men in the forest, the game of chess, and the two curses aimed at his mother's womb: one for bad luck and one for good. The second curse was designed to negate the first, and it might have worked that way, except for the one complication that nobody expected: *There were two babies in the womb.*

"Yes," he said. "I know what happened. I mean, I do now. I finally understand." There were a thousand things he had to tell her and a hundred things he wanted to know, but this wasn't the time. "If we can, we have to get out of here," he said.

"But how did you get in? The only one who has the keys is—"

"I'll tell you later. Right now, let's just take a look outside and see if we can sneak away."

"I can't," she said, pointing to her ankle. The chain

ended in a manacle, held in place by a padlock.

"Don't worry about that," Tom said. He used the key to unlock the manacle, and felt a stir of anger when he saw the bruised and welted skin the metal cuff left behind. He noticed her staring wide-eyed at the key, which was still rapidly changing its shape, over and over. She looked dazed, but he couldn't blame her. Out of the blue, her long-lost brother had turned up with a glowing toad and a magic key. "I'll explain all this later," he said. She nodded, still gawking.

They went to the door, and Tom opened it a crack. He saw a group of Marauders heading straight for the palanquin, and almost yelped aloud. He pulled the door shut as fast as he dared.

"What?" said the girl, squeezing his shoulder.

"Men are coming," he whispered.

"Lock it again!" she said.

Of course, Tom thought. He fumbled for the key and leaned down, not bothering to take the strap off his head. A moment after he turned the first key, someone tugged at the door from the other side.

A voice bellowed. "What are you doing, trying to open that?"

"Shaddup! Thought I saw something!" another voice barked back.

"Big Boss might be in there," said the first voice.

"The boss ain't here! Don't you think he would've said something by now?"

"Quiet, you! You and your men just keep an eye on this box till we find that spy that got past the fires."

Tom heard heavy footsteps outside every wall of the palanquin as the Marauders surrounded it. He stared at his sister. "That's me they're looking for. We're not going anywhere for a while."

She nodded and reached out to clasp his hands again. Tom marveled once more at how good it felt just to be able to touch another human being. Despite the surrounding danger, he felt a warmth fill his chest and a smile widen his face. "Your name," he said, loud enough for her to hear but soft enough that it would not reach outside the walls. "Is it Alexandra?"

"That's right!" she cried. "And you're Alexander."

"No," he said. "My name is Tom."

Alexandra frowned. "It was Alexander when you were born."

"I know. But the people who took me in didn't know that."

"So how do you know my—" She paused to think, twitching her nose, and then she gasped, squeezing his hand so hard that he winced. "That means you found our father! He must have told you my name!"

Tom smiled despite the pain and nodded. Then, with nothing else to do but wait, they whispered to each other and laughed and wept as they shared their amazing news, both good and bad. Alexandra used a tinderbox to light the candle again as she spoke. Tom's heart was pierced when she told him that their mother had been mortally wounded during the invasion of the Marauders, and the two servants that carried the twins away had somehow been separated in the confused escape, never to reunite. Irmel, the woman who raised Alexandra, had told her about her lost twin, and she knew the story of the dual curses.

"I can't believe you found our father! I can't wait to meet him," she whispered. Her eyes glimmered, and she sniffed back tears. "Tell me about him!"

That's the difference between us. You've never had a father, Tom thought. He couldn't help but compare her pure joy with his apprehension. "Yes, I'll tell you. But first I want to know: How did you get here? Were you stolen by the Marauders?" Tom asked.

"Yes! Months ago, they came and took me from poor old Irmel. They must have heard that I bring good luck. It was that horrible—"

Tom put a finger to his lips as he heard shouting outside. "Hey, Big Boss is here!" a Marauder cried.

"It's him," Alexandra said, shrinking back.

"Who?" asked Tom.

"That horrible little gnome. They call him Big Boss. But I've heard another name for him, too: Stiltskin."

"*S*tiltskin?" cried Tom, almost too loud. He covered his own mouth with his hand. Outside the palanquin he heard a familiar voice, sharp and grating.

"What's the matter with all of ye? Shet yer mouths, and get that look off yer faces!"

Tom felt like he couldn't breathe. He put a palm against the wall to keep from falling. *Is it Rumpel-Stiltskin? Is my gnome the leader of the Marauders? How can this be?*

"Come here," said Alexandra, pulling him toward the side of the palanquin opposite her bed. "There's a crack in the wall, we might be able to see!"

Tom found the narrow gap, a long slit between two of the boards on the side of the palanquin. He and his sister peered through, side by side. There was a fire nearby, and a group of Marauders gathered around it, all staring at someone that Tom couldn't see. Their heads were slowly turning in unison, and Tom knew whoever it was would walk into sight soon enough. He felt dizzy, as if all the air had been used up in the palanquin. And there, coming around the fire, was a tiny figure with a fat belly, spindly arms and legs, and a long filthy beard that nearly reached the ground. It wasn't a pointed hat on top of the head, though. It was a gaudy crown, encrusted with glittering jewels. The gnome slowly limped around, leaning heavily on a staff as if every step was causing him terrible pain.

The gnome spoke, and the voice was familiar. "What's going on here? Is it true, the quill-beast has run off? Well, of course it is, ye worthless monkeys, I can see that with my own eyes. But look at ye, cringing like a bunch of sniveling children! What are ye afraid of? Haven't I led ye to victory and riches, every step along the way?"

"But something went bad—nothing *ever* goes bad! Look what happened to Melch!" a Marauder said, pointing with his sword toward the ruined body on the ground.

"SHET YER MOUTH!" roared the gnome, stepping closer, where Tom could see him better. Tom squinted, trying to take in every detail. And when he looked closer, he saw that this wasn't Rumpel-Stiltskin at all. The resemblance was close, but there were differences. This gnome's hair was streaked with bits of black hair, where Rumpel-Stiltskin had none. The nose was just as bent and crooked, but not as long. And one of this gnome's eyes was frosted over with white.

"It's the other one—the brother!" Tom whispered.

"What other one? What do you mean?" asked Alexandra.

"Did you know it was a pair of gnomes that put the

spells on us?" Tom said, turning away from the crack for a moment. Alexandra nodded. "That's one of them," Tom said. "It has to be. There are two Stiltskins—Rumpel-Stiltskin, and this one, whatever his name is!"

He peered again through the crack in the wall. The gnome mumbled to himself and tugged at his beard. He sneered at the wounded men and the dead body of Melch. Then his gaze fell on the palanquin. Tom held his breath. It seemed as if the gnome was staring at him, although it was impossible to be seen through the tiny crack.

The gnome started to hobble toward the palanquin.

"Oh no . . . he thinks something's wrong. He's coming to check on you!" Tom said.

"Hide—behind the curtain!"

Tom picked up the glow-toad, dove onto the bed, pulled the curtain shut, and stuffed the glow-toad under a blanket. Then his blood stopped flowing in his veins. *The three locks—I only did the top one!*

He pushed the curtain aside and ran softly to the door, pulling out the key. He could hear the slow approach of the gnome—the sharp stab of the staff in the earth, the clump of a boot, and the scrape of the leg that he dragged behind him.

"Hurry!" whispered Alexandra.

Tom turned the middle lock and brought the key down to secure the bottom one. The thumping, scraping steps came to a stop on the other side of the door. He heard a jingle of keys on a chain, and a ring of metal from the opposite side, as he slid his own key into the third lock.

A trickle of sweat rolled down Tom's forehead. If he turned the lock now, the gnome would be sure to hear it and feel it. *Unless . . .*

He felt the top lock in motion, and turned his key at the same time.

On the other side of the door, the gnome grumbled, "Huh?"

No. You didn't notice anything. Just your imagination, Tom thought, stepping cautiously back from the door. He crept past Alexandra, whose eyes looked ready to pop out of her head and go careening off the walls, and jumped into the bed. The door to the palanquin opened as he pulled the curtain shut, and he had to cut himself off from warning his sister about the final problems that he'd just seen: the manacle that should have been around her ankle was lying open on the floor. And the glow-toad's jar was in pieces.

Tom held his breath and listened. There was a shuffling sound as the gnome clambered into the palanquin, and two sharp raps. *Banging his staff on the floor,* Tom figured.

"What's going on in here?" the gnome demanded.

"Nothing," Alexandra said.

"What are ye doing awake?"

"As if I could sleep with all that commotion outside! What's the matter with your precious army that they scare so easily?"

The gnome snorted and grumbled to himself. Tom heard the muttering voice turn his way. If the gnome decided to look behind the curtain, it was over for him. He bunched his hand into a fist, ready to land at least one punch if that happened, right on the spindly nose.

"Well," the gnome said sourly, "get to bed. Can't have my precious charm losing her sleep. Got to keep ye healthy."

"Just leave me alone, you horrible little creature," snapped Alexandra. "That's the best thing you can do for me."

"Watch yer mouth, little one," the gnome said. It sounded like he was limping toward the door. "There'll come a time when I don't need ye anymore. And ye know what happens then." He made a horrible choking sound, followed by a nasty chuckle. The door opened and closed, the three locks clicked, and the footsteps moved off. Tom sucked in a huge gulp of air and pulled the curtain back.

Smart girl, he thought, when he saw what she'd done. Alexandra had stepped right over the open manacle and the shattered jar, covering them with the simple gown that she was wearing. Before he could pay her a compliment, though, he heard the gnome shouting outside.

"Know what ye boys need? Some entertainment, that's what! Bring me the prisoner!"

"Now what?" Tom said, returning to the crack in the wall. He thought back to the sight of the hooded prisoner being led up the hill, and an uneasy thought crept into his head. *There was something familiar about that prisoner . . . I didn't want to think about it, but there was.*

"Ye there—fetch the wheel," Stiltskin ordered, sweeping his large hand into an arc. Four of his soldiers jogged away, beyond where the narrow slit allowed Tom to see. They came back shortly, carrying something that looked like a wide wagon wheel mounted flat on a pedestal.

"Not this again . . . I can't watch," whispered Alexandra, shaking her head.

"Why? What's that wheel for?" asked Tom. His teeth closed painfully tight on his lower lip. He pressed his face against the slit to widen his view, and spotted the prisoner being hauled toward the wheel and into the light of the fire. One of the Marauders reached for the prisoner's hood and pulled it off.

"No," Tom whispered.

"What?" said Alexandra. "Who is that man?"

Tom turned away from the slit to stare at her. "That's our father."

Conrad was shoved and pulled toward the wheel. When he saw the gnome standing there with the fire casting a devilish light over his tiny misshapen form, his body twitched from head to toe. Then he set his jaw and stared fiercely down at Stiltskin.

Stiltskin glared back up at Conrad and pointed a crooked finger. "Ye . . . I've met ye before, haven't I?"

Conrad straightened up, rising even higher over the

bent figure of the gnome. "You have. In a forest, long ago."

Stiltskin tilted his head to one side and yanked at his beard. Then he snickered and slapped a knee with his enormous hand. "Ha! I remember! The good-for-nothing who meddled in my game of chess and ruined my victory! Fancy the fate that brought ye here. . . . Well, it's a different game we'll play today, my foolish friend!"

Conrad watched uneasily as a group of Marauders carried the wheel over and put it between him and Stiltskin. The gnome reached down, gripped the wheel with an oversized hand, and spun it. The wheel creaked and whirred as it twirled, until Stiltskin pressed his boot against the rim to make it stop. There were ten spokes on the wheel, and Tom saw round holes drilled into the rim, one at every spoke.

Another Marauder came forward, bearing a tray with ten glasses of red liquid, and a vial.

"Ten cups of wine," Stiltskin said, gesturing. "And one vial of poison." He turned to the man holding the tray. "Do it," he said. The man with the tray turned his back to the rest of them. He lifted the vial high so it could be seen over his shoulder. Then he lowered the vial. When he lifted the hand again, the vial was upside down and empty.

"He's poisoned one of the glasses," Alexandra said. Her voice quavered. "I've seen him play this game before. Stiltskin never . . . the prisoner always . . ." She couldn't finish the thought. Tom groped for her hand and squeezed it.

"Give the tray to our guest," said Stiltskin with an unpleasant grin. The man handed the tray to Conrad. Tom saw Conrad's throat bob up and down as he swallowed.

"What do I do with this?" Conrad said in a thin, high voice.

"Put one in every spoke," Stiltskin said. "Any way ye want. So ye know it's an honest game."

"I . . . I don't want to," Conrad said.

Instantly, a Marauder behind Conrad drew a sword and prodded him in the back. "Do like Big Boss says," the Marauder said, growling. Conrad winced and began to place the ten glasses in the ten holes at the end of the ten spokes. Even from this distance, through the slit, Tom could see beads of sweat on Conrad's brow. Hundreds of Marauders gathered around to watch, encircling the wheel. Tom could barely see over their heads.

"It's a game of *luck*," Stiltskin said, cracking the knuckles on each hand. "Spin the wheel, then drink the wine that stops before ye. If ye lose, I get the pleasure of watching ye die. If I lose, ye get the pleasure of watching *me* die, and then ye'll be set free." Stiltskin's eyes gleamed. He lowered his head and stared like a wolf. He didn't look like he expected to lose.

Conrad put the last glass in place and let the tray clatter to the ground. "I don't like games of chance. I like games of skill. How about chess instead? Surely you remember how to play. I'll even take my queen off the board, to give you the advantage. How about it, sir?"

Stiltskin inclined his head and smiled wickedly. "It's not up to the captor to choose the game. Now spin the wheel. I'll even risk the first drink—so the odds will favor *ye*, my friend."

Tom saw Conrad close his eyes and whisper something to himself. The sword prodded Conrad's back again, and he grunted with pain. He reached down, grabbed the rim of the wheel—awkwardly, with both hands still bound together—and spun it.

"What do we do?" Alexandra said into Tom's ear as the glasses whirled by. She still clutched his hand. "We have to do *something*!"

"Let me think," said Tom. He saw Stiltskin glance back at the palanquin, and smirk. Tom fought to control his careening thoughts, and realized there might be something he could do after all. "Stiltskin always wins because he keeps you nearby, closer to him than the other fellow. So if you . . ."

"Get away, and let you stay closer!" Alexandra said.

"Too late this time," Tom replied. The wheel squeaked and slowed to a stop. With utter confidence, Stiltskin lifted the glass that had landed before him. He raised the glass to Conrad in a mock salute. Then he tipped it into his open mouth, licked his lips, wiped his sleeve across the mouth, and replaced the glass with a grin.

"Yer turn," Stiltskin said, pointing at the glass in front of Conrad.

"Oh no," Alexandra said. She squeezed Tom's hand so hard, he thought the fingers might break. Tom watched his father lift the glass from its hole. The hands trembled and the wine inside sloshed as he raised it.

"Drink up," Stiltskin said, stroking his chin.

Conrad closed his eyes and paused with his lips pressed tight together. Then he opened his mouth and poured the wine down his throat. *It's like Hazard*, Tom thought. *A game of chance. What are the odds now? Nine glasses left, and one was poisoned. That can't be the poison Conrad just drank. . . . Don't let it be the one!* "Please. Don't die, Father," Tom whispered, letting the word slip out without regret.

Conrad kept his head tilted back for a moment, and seemed to waver on his feet. He blinked, and looked around in surprise.

"He's all right. Alexandra, we evened the odds!" Tom said. "Now we—" He stopped midquestion as he saw Stiltskin turn back to stare at the palanquin.

"Is there a problem, old friend?" Conrad said, sensing that something had unsettled the leader of the Marauders.

Stiltskin snapped his head back to glare at Conrad, his lip curled high on one side. "No! Not a thing," the gnome said. "Spin again!"

This time it was Conrad who glanced at the palanquin, and Tom was sure he'd seen a glimmer of hope in his father's eyes. Conrad reached down and spun the wheel again, much harder this time. It squealed and screeched as it turned.

"Get back," Tom said to Alexandra. "To the other side, as far as you can get!" He felt a lump in his throat, and his face grew hot. Alexandra ran to the back of the palanquin and pressed herself in the farthest corner. She closed her eyes and turned away, putting her face to the wall, as if to minimize her presence.

Tom peered through the crack. The wheel stopped with full glasses in front of Stiltskin and Conrad. Stiltskin lifted his glass and peered nervously over his shoulder. The glass shook in his hand. Tom glared through the slot, leaning against the wall with his fists bunched tight and his lips pressed together.

"Ye first this time," the gnome said to Conrad.

Conrad took his glass without hesitating, downed it, and slammed the empty vessel back into the hole in the wheel. He stared at the gnome. "Now *ye*, my friend," he said with a thin smile.

Three gone. Seven left, Tom thought. *One poison . . .* That familiar sensation appeared in his head, as if something was tickling the inside of his skull.

The gnome's gnarly face filled with fear and hate. He glared at the Marauders that surrounded him, and raised the trembling glass to his lips. He tilted his head back, opened his mouth, and poured in the wine.

Stiltskin wiped his sleeve across his mouth, belched, and grinned. He reached down, and Tom thought he was going to spin the wheel again. But his legs buckled underneath him. The gnome gripped the wheel with one hand. Then he dropped his staff, and both hands went to his throat, burrowing through his beard to grip his neck. He spun halfway about, and Tom could see the good eye swirling madly. The gnome gasped and opened his mouth as if to retch, but nothing came out. He dropped to his knees, doubled over at the waist, and then rolled onto his side and moved no more.

All around him the Marauders stared in silence. "That's not supposed to happen," one of them cried. And then someone screamed. A gasping, openmouthed Marauder staggered out of the group, reaching behind him with both hands as if to clasp them behind his back. He turned, and Tom saw an arrow lodged between his shoulders.

Two more Marauders shrieked and fell. Tom saw deadly arrows in graceful flight, catching slivers of moonlight and falling into the crowd. The Marauders scrambled like a colony of ants whose sheltering rock had just been pried from the ground. "We're being attacked!"

"It's our father's army," Tom cried. "They're coming!" He leaped up and down twice, and then put his eye back to the slit, thinking suddenly of his father's safety. Conrad had taken advantage of the chaos to dive under the wheel unnoticed. He crawled beneath it and sprang up on the other side, then ran to one of the fallen Marauders. He held the dead man's sword between his knees and used it to slice through the ropes that bound his hands. Arrows were falling like rain. Tom saw one soar right past his father's ear.

"He'll get killed out there!" Tom cried. He ran to the door, used the key to open the three locks, and swung it wide open. Before he could step out and call to his father, Alexandra darted under his arm and out the door. She ran toward Conrad. "Stop!" Tom shouted, and he was going to follow her until he realized what she was doing—and why it had to be her that went.

Conrad wielded the sword, looking for someone to fight despite the peril of the arrows. When he saw the redheaded girl dashing toward him, a look of pure bewilderment overcame over his face and the sword slipped out of his hand. He didn't resist as she seized his hand and pulled him toward the palanquin. As they ran together, arrows fell from the sky and landed to the left and right of Conrad, never touching him. Alexandra was using her luck to shield him from harm. Tom stepped back to let them in, and closed the door behind them.

Conrad stood with his chest heaving and his eyes gleaming, looking from one of them to the other. He reached out and put a palm beside each of their faces. Alexandra smiled up at him.

"I guess you know who she is," Tom said.

Conrad nodded.

"It all makes sense now. Doesn't it, Father?" Tom said.

Conrad wavered a bit, smiled, and nodded again. Then he put a hand on their shoulders and pulled them close, crushing them against his chest. Tom wrapped an arm around them both, and Alexandra did likewise, and the three of them stood there, rocking slowly back and forth like the great willows of Londria in a gentle morning breeze. Tom was dimly aware of the shouting outside, the woeful cries of pain, the crashing of metal, and the thumping of boots and hooves as the Marauders grabbed whatever loot they could carry and ran, afraid once more of the men of Londria and no longer under the protection of the mysterious gnome and his strange good fortune.

24

Tom and Alexandra sat side by side on the hilltop with their elbows across their knees, and waited for the sun to rise over the top of the forest. The attack in the night had become a rout, and the invading army was shattered and dispersed. Every one of the Marauders was dead or on the run. Many tried to carry too much of the plunder away with them. Slowed by the weight, they felt the sting of Londrian arrows in their backs, and the loot was scattered in front of their fallen bodies.

Tom watched with admiration as his father took charge once more. The whole night, Conrad's spirit had flagged only once—when he learned from Alexandra that his beloved wife had perished years before. He'd walked away and sat by himself to watch the moon drop from the sky, and waved away anyone who tried to come near. "It's a cruel loss," he said to Tom and Alexandra when he came back. "But look at everything I've found."

Before the night was over, Conrad had the wagons loaded with the plunder once again. He divided the men into groups so that they could escort every wagon back to one of the ruined towns to try to restore the wealth to those who had lost it. "It will be a messy undertaking. There's no way to tell what came from what town, but we'll be as fair as we can. I will take the wagon back to Penwall," Conrad told the others, turning briefly to smile at his children.

Alexandra reached for Tom's hand and squeezed it. "I'll go with you," she said. "I'll ask our father to send word to Irmel that I'm all right. But I'll stay with you from now on, Tom. So you don't have to be alone."

Tom saw the sun appear, oozing like molten gold over the tops of the trees. He felt the warmth of the first rays on his face. "You would do that for me?"

Alexandra nodded.

"But you'll want your own life someday," Tom said. "You can't just be stuck by my side forever."

His sister gave him a gentle punch on the shoulder. "I can if I want. I'm going wherever you go."

"Not everywhere," he said quietly.

She looked at him from the corner of her eyes and nodded, understanding what he meant. "Yes, *everywhere*," she said. "Even there. Do you think you'll see Rumpel-Stiltskin in the Dark Dell, like he said?"

"I guess so," Tom said. "And maybe he'll end my curse, like he promised."

"Then I'm definitely coming with you. I want him to end my curse too," she said.

Tom leaned away and stared at her. That was a thought that had never occurred to him. "But . . . people don't hate the way you are. Why would you want that?"

Alexandra stiffened. She pointed toward the palanquin. "That awful gnome and the Marauders kept me a prisoner for months because of the good luck I brought them. And you know what terrible things they were able to do because of me. Do you think I ever want that to happen again? It would, Tom. Irmel was always afraid of something like that. She thought it would be some baron or prince, or the king himself who'd come and steal me and keep me like a bird in a cage for the luck I'd bring. So we lived in the hills, hoping nobody would ever find us. But that horrible Stiltskin learned about me, somehow. And then he . . ."

Tom looked at her, wondering why her voice had trailed off. "What is it?" he asked.

Alexandra stared at the ground near the wheel that was used to play the deadly game. "Where is he? Where's the gnome?"

Tom stood to get a better look, and she got up with him. They walked side by side to the wheel.

"This is where he fell," Tom said. "I'm sure of it."

But the body of the gnome was gone.

25

Four horses drew the wagon toward Penwall. Tom and Alexandra sat on a bench behind the driver, careful to keep the same distance between themselves and him. Behind them a wide canvas was strapped tight over the bulging pile of plunder, hiding it from curious eyes. Two dozen armed men—Tom was happy to see Jordan and Rolf among them—escorted the wagon to discourage any thieves or straggling Marauders from attacking, and Conrad rode ahead of all of them. Not a minute would go by before Conrad would turn to wink or smile or wave at his son and daughter, and sometimes he would shake his head as if he could scarcely believe they'd all come together. Tom knew the feeling well.

The road began to look familiar, and Tom realized that Penwall was near. He stood on the bench with a hand on Alexandra's shoulder to steady him, trying to see what lay ahead.

"I hope they're here," Alexandra said.

Tom's voice hitched when he replied, "Me too." Penwall was the first place to look for his parents, to be sure. Maybe, after the Marauders had come and gone, his mum and dad had returned to the ruins of their town. But then something terrible occurred to Tom, and his head went numb. *What if they went looking for me on my island? And then when I wasn't there, they went who-knows-where to try to find me? How will I find them then?* He shook his head like a rattle, trying to cast off that notion.

In the forest near Penwall, he saw men cutting down trees, and teams of horses pulling the wood toward the town. They passed blackened timbers, discarded in a heap. Tom heard the rasp of saws and the clatter of hammers.

"Look, they're rebuilding already," Conrad called back. "Aren't people grand? Knock them down, and they'll pick themselves up first chance they get." He looked at the town, nodding to himself, and then called to Tom again. "Tom—the names of your folks, it was Gilbert and Joan Holly, wasn't it?"

Tom nodded. Conrad spurred his horse and rode ahead.

The wagon stopped at the edge of town, and curious people came out to see why the soldiers had come and what news they had. Tom craned his neck, trying to see where Conrad had gone, and searched the crowd for his mother and father. *Father*, he said to himself. Could a boy have two fathers—the one who made him and the one who raised him—and love them both? *Sure he can,* Tom thought.

Tom saw Conrad, still on his horse, speak to a pair of people and point toward the wagon. The two came dashing down the street: a slight, tall man, pulling a short, plump woman behind him. Tom let out a whoop and leaped off the cart.

"Hey! Not without me, remember?" Alexandra cried, jumping down behind him.

Gilbert and Joan Holly ran up, round-eyed, red-faced, and puffing, and stopped the usual twenty paces away. "Tom, Tom!" they shouted together, bouncing as if their shoes had springs. Gilbert put his hands over his heart, as if it might burst out of his chest otherwise. Joan clapped her hands over her mouth, but her smile was so wide it could not be concealed. For a moment, they stared only at him. Then their eyes were drawn to the red-haired girl by his side.

"This is my sister, Mum and Dad," Tom said. "Alexandra."

Gilbert stared at her, and at Tom again. A notion seemed to pop into his head, and he turned to look at the red-haired man on the horse, trotting up behind them.

"Yes, I'm his father," Conrad said, anticipating the question. He bowed in the saddle. "We'll tell you all about it in a moment. But for now, all you need to know is that you may hug your boy once more. So long as that precious girl is by his side."

Tom didn't wait for the news to sink in. He ran to his parents, pulling Alexandra behind him, and rushed into them so quickly that they all fell into a laughing, weeping heap in the middle of the road.

It was the beginning of the happiest night of Tom's young life. While the people of Penwall gathered around, Conrad pulled the canvas off the wagon and revealed the riches that were being returned. Tom's heart warmed when he saw the amazement on their faces. It was a night for celebrating, thanksgiving, laughing, and dancing. It was a night for warm embraces that were long denied. And it was a night for the telling of astounding stories, although the only magical evidence that Tom could offer was the plump glow-toad, nestled comfortably in the new box Tom had found for its home.

But not everything was perfect. Tom could see that something troubled Gilbert. Whenever Conrad was near, Gilbert fell silent. Once, from a distance, Tom watched Conrad approach Gilbert, and shake his hand warmly and speak to him. Gilbert nodded, and it looked like he said "thank you." He smiled in a half-hearted way, but when Conrad turned and walked away, Gilbert's mouth flattened into a thin, horizontal line. Joan knew something was wrong because she went to Gilbert and patted his arm, and whispered into his ear.

There was another matter that tempered the joy for Tom. It was the knowledge that very soon, he must venture into the Dark Dell once more, to fulfill a promise made to the ornery gnome who'd made all this possible. And there he would see if a pair of curses might be broken at last.

26

Tom was far from alone on the journey to the Dark Dell. Alexandra, who had inherited even more of Conrad's stubborn streak than Tom, refused to leave his side. Conrad would not let his newfound children out of his sight, and thought it best to bring a few more armed men with them for safety. Jordan and Rolf were quick to volunteer. Gilbert Holly insisted on coming as well— and even spoke sharply to Conrad when it was suggested that it wasn't necessary—and it was only after much pleading that Tom managed to convince his worried mother to remain behind.

There were five horses for the six of them, to speed the journey. Tom and Alexandra rode together. Along the way, Tom watched Conrad trot up to Gilbert more than once, to try to strike up a conversation. But Gilbert seemed wary of this strapping redheaded warrior. His jaw ground from side to side, and he rarely responded to Conrad with more than a single word or a grunt. Also, it seemed that Gilbert tried again and again to maneuver his horse to put himself between Conrad and the children. The behavior was almost rude, and utterly unlike the affable gracious Gilbert Holly that Tom had known nearly all his life. Conrad noticed the demeanor too. Once, Tom caught him casting a troubled look at Gilbert.

"What's going on between those two?" Tom whispered to Alexandra.

"I haven't the slightest notion," Alexandra replied.

When Tom wasn't keeping an uneasy eye on his two fathers, he watched the brush beside the road, searching for the dark glumberries that would get them past the vicious Nippers that guarded the mouth of the Dark Dell. Finally, with none of the berries in sight along the roadside, he had to retrace his steps all the way back to the thorny bush on the ledge, near the gnome's dismal hideaway. He and Alexandra picked the bush clean of the few berries that were left.

Tom paused outside the narrow entrance that led to the dismal chamber. "Rumpel-Stiltskin used to live in there," he told Alexandra.

"Would you like to go inside? Maybe he's in there."

Tom shook his head. "No. I don't want to see that again. And he told me where to find him. It's not here; it's in the Dark Dell."

Standing there reminded Tom of something he ought to do. He took off his pack and dug out a wooden box. When he lifted the lid, the glow-toad was there, gleaming softly, as complacent as always. "You're home, little toad. This is where I found you." Tom lifted it from the box and put it gently on the ground. He patted the warty head, and then nudged the toad on the rear with two fingers. It took a single hop into the stony passage. "Thank you for the light," Tom said. "I couldn't have made it without you."

The glow-toad twisted its body to look back at Tom with its round, watery eyes. Then it turned itself around, hopped back to the box, and rose on its hind legs, trying to heave itself over the edge and back inside. Alexandra giggled.

"Fine," Tom said, grinning. "I guess I'll keep you for a while after all."

The path narrowed and the stony hills crept closer on either side. Rolf and Jordan, who'd heard of the fearsome reputation of the Dark Dell, eyed the hills warily. Gilbert Holly fidgeted and gnawed at his fingernails, until he seemed to notice how Conrad looked—as calm as if he was going to the town fair. Gilbert cleared his throat, tightly grasped his reins with both hands, and straightened his back.

"We're almost there," Tom said quietly to Alexandra.

"What are you supposed to do?" she asked.

Tom shrugged. "I really don't know. All he told me was that I should go back to the Dark Dell, and he'd try to fix my curse. So I guess we'll find out when we're in there." A shiver coursed through his shoulders, as he thought of the quill-beasts and their dreadful faces. *And what happens if one of those things comes after us?*

They came around a bend, and the slender valley was before them. Just ahead, Tom saw the ancient rockfall that nearly shut the dell off from the rest of the world.

"Just so you know, there's a warning written with stones," Tom called ahead to the others.

"Is there really?" said Conrad, turning around. His eyebrows were high, and his mouth was tightened into a little circle.

"Yes. It says 'trespass and die,'" said Tom.

Conrad waited for Tom and Alexandra to ride up beside him, and he pointed at the ground. "That's not all it says."

Tom stared down at the fat stones arranged on the ground. The original warning was still there: TRES-PASS AND DIE. But now a second message was beside it: ENTER RED HAIR.

Tom stared at the words. The stones that formed them were huge. It had to be the work of the quill-beast.

"Looks like you've made a friend, Son," said Gilbert.

CHAPTER

27

There weren't enough glumberries to treat them all. Tom and Alexandra both had to go into the dell so that anyone who went with them would be safe from Tom's bad luck. And besides, Alexandra was just as keen as her brother to shed her curse. Once Tom and Alexandra had stained themselves with the juice, it was clear that there were only enough berries left for one more. It was decided that Rolf and Jordan would stay to watch the horses. But Conrad and Gilbert began to argue, and the tone grew so bitter that it made Tom's stomach hurt to listen.

"Please, Gilbert," Conrad said. "If there's danger in there, who should be with the children—a fighter or a toymaker?"

"Listen, I may not be able to swing a sword like you, but that doesn't mean I want Tom to walk into danger without me," Gilbert said, glaring at the bigger man.

"You saw the message in stone," Conrad said sharply, pointing. "It said 'enter red hair.' What if the creatures meant just that? Red-haired folk?"

"Oh, is that what you think? That it's your family now,

and that red mane of yours is all that counts? You may have given him the red hair, sir, but he's been my boy for the last ten years!"

Tom could hardly breathe in the tense, silent moment that followed. Gilbert crossed his arms and stared, and Conrad put his fists on his hips and thrust his jaw forward. It was Conrad who finally took a deep breath, shut his eyes for a moment, and then quietly spoke. "I see. Yes, I understand. Gilbert . . . please. Walk with me for a moment. I believe we need a word alone."

It was more than a moment; it seemed like an hour. Tom watched Gilbert, with a sullen expression, wander off and talk to Conrad, too far away for him or Alexandra to overhear. After a while the two men sat in the grass and talked some more. Finally Conrad reached out with his right hand and Gilbert took it. They shook hands and helped each other to their feet. Tom's spirits lifted when he saw Gilbert smiling—a genuine smile this time.

"Tom," Gilbert said, "Conrad will take you and your sister into the Dark Dell. I have to admit, you'll be safer with him to guard you. I'll wait here for you. Be careful, Son. Come back to me." He reached down and ruffled Tom's hair. "You too, young lady," he said to Alexandra. She put her arms around Gilbert's waist and squeezed.

"You have the loveliest freckles," Gilbert told her, smoothing her red hair.

"Thank you, Gilbert," Conrad said, putting a hand on

Gilbert's shoulder. "Now, children—pass me the berries."

Three redheaded people, a man and his children, climbed over the rockfall, where they saw the Dark Dell revealed at last: a deep, verdant cleft in the hills with waterfalls thundering down sheer cliffs on either side. The shallow swamp was directly below them, and Tom scowled when he remembered the ferocious insects that lurked there.

He saw a dead bird on the ground, with tiny red wounds all over its black-feathered body. *Nippers*, Tom thought. It reminded him of the awful story the gnome had told him a few nights before, about the bird that chose not to fly and simply folded its wings and fell to its doom. That was a tale he hoped he'd be able to someday forget.

"Ready?" Conrad asked.

Tom nodded. He saw the grim look on Alexandra's face as she stared at the placid waters. "We'll be all right," he told her. "The glumberries will keep us safe."

"Tom, do you mind going first? Then Alexandra. I'll stay behind where I can see both of you," Conrad said. He drew his sword as if it might be useful against a swarm of ravenous, leaping bugs.

Tom led the way across the swamp, stepping from stone to knoll to stone. He expected countless Nippers to fill the air, like they'd done before. But nothing bounded out of the tall grass, and the water was as calm and reflective as a mirror.

"Are you sure this is that pond?" Alexandra whispered as if she was afraid the little creatures would hear.

"I'm sure," Tom replied. He was delighted not to see them—even with the protection of the berries, he'd received painful, feverish bites the last time he crossed this way. But still, he wondered why the Nippers were leaving them alone. Was there a difference in the weather? The time of day? The ripeness of the berries? Whatever the reason, he was glad of it, especially when they all stood on dry ground again.

"Nothing to it," Conrad said. He looked at something across the swamp, and Tom turned and saw Gilbert Holly standing on top of the distant rockfall with his hand held high. Tom waved back.

"I was wondering," Tom said to Conrad. "What did you say to my dad just now? I mean . . . my other dad. Is everything all right?"

Conrad leaned over and put his hands on his knees, so he could look Tom in the eye. "I said a lot of things, Tom. I told him that I was amazed at the job he and his wife did raising such a smart, brave, good-hearted boy. You wouldn't have survived this adventure if they didn't bring you up right. And I promised him that I'm not here to claim you for my own, even if I am your blood father. I said you probably wouldn't allow that to happen, anyway, being the boy you are. I only asked him for one thing, Tom. I said I want to be part of your life from now on. And I want Alexandra to be part of our lives, too. Yours and mine. As long as that's what you want."

Tom felt a warmth fill him, starting in his head and rushing down to the tips of his fingers and toes. "Yes, sir," he said. "That's what I want."

They hid behind trees and cautiously peered out. The fence was in front of them, and then the meadow where sheep and cows ambled. Past that, the huge house was nestled snug against the side of the cliff. White smoke wafted from the chimney. *Looks like someone's home*, Tom thought.

"That door must be twelve feet high," said Conrad, fingering the hilt of his sword.

"I think I should go alone," Tom said.

"I think not," Conrad replied, arching one brow. "Listen, Tom, the instructions this gnome left you were sort of vague. 'Meet me back in the Dark Dell.' That doesn't necessarily mean you should walk up and knock on that door."

"But the message written in stone . . ." Tom said, raising his palms.

"Tom, the creature in there—the *creatures*, I mean— can stop a man's heart with their faces. I realize you did them a great service, but what if they're not as happy to see you as you think? Besides, it's the gnome you're looking for. Not the quill-beasts."

"I have a thought," Alexandra said. Conrad and Tom

turned to look at her. She cleared her throat and tugged at the sleeve of her dress. "Tom, Rumpel-Stiltskin never let anyone see him except you. Isn't that right?"

Tom thought back through all his adventures. He was surprised to realize that it was true. No one else had laid eyes on the gnome, not once. "Yes. That's right. He did his vanishing trick as soon as anyone else turned up."

"Why, do you suppose?"

"We know why: He's a criminal. There's a price on his head," Conrad said.

"Maybe," Alexandra said. "Or maybe there's another reason he's shy. Perhaps he hasn't shown up because someone's been with Tom, ever since he found me. Maybe Tom needs to go off by himself for a moment."

Tom was already nodding. It made perfect sense. "Of course. It's worth a try. I'll just walk over there, through those trees, until I'm out of sight."

Conrad's brow was furrowed. He stared in the direction that Tom intended to take, and then looked keenly at Tom. "Not too far, Tom. And give a shout if anything's amiss."

Tom walked along the edge of the woods until he was sure the others couldn't see him, and then took another hundred steps, just to be sure. There was a fat round boulder, and he sat on it and waited. He looked in the shadows of the trees and up at the limbs overhead, but the gnome wasn't there.

"Rumpel-Stiltskin!" he called. He climbed onto the boulder and turned in a circle as he spoke. "Can you hear me? I came back to the Dark Dell, like you asked. And I did the thing you wanted me to do. I helped beat the Marauders! You remember our bargain, don't you? You said you'd end my curse if I did that for you. And I know you can end it, because you're the one who did this to me in the first place! So do it! Come here, and *end my curse!*"

There was no sign or sound of the gnome, just the breeze whistling in the branches overhead and a cowbell in the pasture beyond the trees.

"He's not here," Tom said to himself. He stood there, tapping his thighs, and made a decision. It was time to knock on the quill-beasts' door. *But I'm doing this alone,* he thought. *In case it isn't safe.*

He hopped off the boulder, threaded through the trees until he stood at the edge of the field, took three deep breaths, and ran. When he reached the fence, he slipped between the railings and ran again. The cows and sheep turned to watch, mildly intrigued. Behind him he heard Alexandra shout: "Tom! Tom, stop!"

No, he thought, *and don't follow me!* He made it to the fence on the other side of the field and climbed it. The house was just ahead, towering high, and he ran into its shadow. He arrived at the door and raised his fist to knock. But before he could strike it, the door opened. A monstrous figure loomed overhead. It was covered with a cloak, a hood over the face. All Tom could see of its hide was the end of the arm that had opened the door. It bristled with lethal quills.

"Welcome, boy," the voice boomed down. "We wondered when you would come." It was the deeper voice Tom had heard in Dram and on the hill where the Marauders were camped. "Tell the others to join you. Silly folk; did you think we didn't see you, skulking about in our woods?"

Conrad walked into the house first, and the only hint of his tension was in the wideness of his eyes and the way his right arm was bent slightly, ready to reach across and grab his sword. He bowed to the two enormous cloaked figures in the room, and they nodded down at him. Alexandra burst in next, dashing around Conrad and attaching herself to Tom's side.

"Welcome, all of you," said the larger quill-beast. "We expected one redhead, who we hoped to thank someday. But here are three."

"You must be Maud," Tom said to the smaller one. "I'm Tom, and this is my sister, Alexandra, and my father, Conrad. I don't know your name, sir," he said to the other quill-beast.

"Call me Anderlin" was the reply.

"I'm glad you made it back here, Anderlin. Now I'm here because . . . someone told me to come. Rumpel-Stiltskin," Tom said.

Maud inclined her hooded head to one side. "You

knew Rum? And he told you to come here? When did he tell you that?"

"Just a few days ago," Tom said. "He told me to meet him in the Dark Dell."

"That cannot be," said Anderlin.

"Why do you say that, sir?" asked Conrad.

The quill-beasts turned toward each other. Then they looked down at Tom.

"Because Rumpel-Stiltskin has been dead for more than a year," said Maud. "He died here, and we buried him in the cave behind this house."

28

Tom stared down at the stone coffin. Not long ago he'd stood in the same cavern where the stone box sat at the edge of the abyss. That time, there was no lamp to see by. In utter darkness, he'd felt the letters inscribed in the lid and tried to trace them with his fingers before the gnome had told him to stop.

Now, in the yellow glow of the lamps that the quill-beasts had set on the stone floor, he could read the letters plainly: RUMPEL-STILTSKIN.

"I don't understand," Tom said. It was the only thing he could think of to say. "Are you sure he's in there?"

"Would you like to see?" asked Maud, reaching for the lid.

"No," Tom replied, without hesitating. Someone's body was in there; he knew that well enough. He could still remember the way the beard crumbled under his touch when he reached for the key. His thoughts swirled and collided, and he searched for a way to make sense of it all. There were things he'd learned during his adventures, memories that didn't fit in. "Wait," he said, turning to Maud. "You said his name that day! You said 'Was it you, Rum? Did you come back?'"

Maud's head tilted down toward him. "So that was *you* that crept into my house," she said. She sounded more amused than angry, but Tom still felt Alexandra's hand close tight around his.

"Um . . . yes," Tom replied. "I'm sorry. But Rum told me to come here that day. . . . Except you say he's dead, so he couldn't have told me that. . . . And you called him by name. . . . Oh, I don't understand any of this."

"I am beginning to," said Maud. "But let me answer your question first. I called his name that day because, even after he died, I felt Rum's presence more than once, with a sense beyond my eyes and ears. I didn't see him, but I was sure his spirit was there, watching me. I thought he was trying to speak to me, though I could not hear the words. But *you* could see him, Tom. And you could hear him."

"Don't tell me . . ." Tom whispered. It was something he already knew but didn't want to hear aloud.

"It was a ghost, Tom," Maud said, telling him anyway. "I've been told that children may see spirits when older folk do not. That must be the answer. Rum needed someone to help him. And so he turned to you: the boy who could see."

Tom needed desperately to sit before he fell, and he almost took a seat on the coffin before gathering his wits. He lowered himself to the floor, and Alexandra sat beside him. "I can't believe this," he said. "It's impossible." But the more he considered it, the more likely it seemed that the impossible might be true.

"Maud, did you know this gnome well?" asked Conrad.

Maud nodded.

"Tell them about our ill-mannered friend, dear," said Anderlin.

Maud crossed her spiny hands, one over the other, and began. "Rumpel-Stiltskin came into the dell more than a year ago, though I did not learn his name at first. I saw him limp along, leaning heavily on his walking stick and moving slowly, with great pain. So I did what I always do when the rare stranger comes into our dell: I howled and showed my face to frighten him away. But this gnome didn't turn. He looked directly at me with no fear in his eyes, only pain and misery. Then he toppled over and was still. I could not wake him, and I could not leave him there. So I brought him into our home, and Anderlin made a bed for him.

"The gnome woke the next day in a foul mood. Of course, I soon learned that it was his *only* mood. You would think that he might have thanked us for saving and caring for him, but instead he cursed at us and called us terrible names."

"That sounds like him, all right," said Tom.

Maud nodded, and Tom had the sense that she might be smiling, if that hidden face was capable of a smile.

"We gave him food and drink, and covered him with blankets when he shivered," she said. "His arms were twisted and frail, and caused him great pain, so I made splints for him out of branches and strips of hide. It was not easy with these thorny hands, but I did what I could to comfort him. Of course he complained about all of it. When he found out that I had bathed him while he slept and washed his clothes, he was furious! I don't think he ever forgave me for that." Maud's shoulders shook under her cloak, and Tom heard something like a laugh. He looked at Alexandra and saw her smiling.

"You may be wondering why we put up with such a cantankerous guest," Maud said.

"Because you liked the company," Tom answered.

"Yes," said Maud, turning her large cloaked head Tom's way. "But it was even more than that. He was the only being we've met that could stand to look us in the eye. And that is something even Anderlin and I cannot do, no matter how much we love each other, such hideous creatures are we. You can't imagine how much that meant to us. Besides, it was good to have someone new to talk to. He amused us, really, the way he railed on and on about things. So no matter how sharp or abusive his words were, we ignored them and brought him what he needed. His weakness and pain made him our prisoner. But a strange thing happened after a few weeks. You see, Rum—that was what I always called him once I learned his name—was experiencing something that was completely alien to him. For the first time in his existence, someone treated him kindly. I would talk to him while I fed him and ask about his life. He was guarded and evasive at first. But finally he told us some of it, always mixing the truth with lies. But we understood well enough. His days were steeped with misery from the beginning. And it was a long, hard life—hundreds of years, at least. He never knew his mother, and his father was wicked and cruel. He had a brother, but they were bitter rivals from the beginning and filled with hate for each other.

"Rum could never let go of the hate. His hard youth made him cruel and selfish. The people he would meet would perceive this, and they would scorn him. And in turn he became even more cruel and selfish. Friendship, courtesy, charity . . . Those were things he'd never learned and could never express, no more than a fish could suddenly breathe the air. He tried to love once, but it ended in disaster."

"I know that story," Tom said, thinking about the miller's daughter who became a queen.

"Do you?" Maud asked. "The tale of the straw and the gold? Poor Rum. When that girl spurned him, his bitterness grew even worse. And his hatred for his own brother boiled over. They had a strange pact, those two. When their father died, he left behind a powerful object: a wizard's staff. The brothers pried it from his dead hands. Each claimed it for his own, but of course neither would agree to let the other have it. They settled the matter in the strangest way: Every seven years, they would meet to play a game of chess, and the winner would take the staff."

"I've seen that staff," Conrad said. "It's made of black wood. With the head of a horned creature carved on top—like ram's horns on a wolf's head."

"Is that so?" Maud said, tilting her head toward Conrad. "It seems you've met these brothers before."

"I interrupted one of those chess games," Conrad said, staring at the abyss. "To my eternal regret."

Maud nodded gently. "I see. But the curious thing about that staff was that, although it was very powerful, neither gnome could use it very well. According to Rum, only a few of the spells they tried to cast actually worked."

At least two of them did, Tom thought.

"The story of that wizard's staff was one of the last things Rum told me about his life," Maud said. "Soon after that he became desperately ill. He was so weak he could hardly move. An unimaginable fever overcame him—so hot that it made the air shimmer over his head! Something strange happened when that sickness took him. Most people turn delirious when such a wicked fever strikes. But for Rum, who spent his life in a sort of madness, the fever brought sudden clarity and sanity. For a long time he simply wept. When he could speak, he said he knew he'd done too much evil in his life. He said he wished he could set things right and make amends for the misery he'd caused. But he despaired, knowing that he was near the end of his days and too weak to leave this house again. 'I'm out of time,' he finally said."

Maud sighed. "Those were the last words he spoke. When I called to him, he didn't answer. When I touched him, he didn't move. The fever had left, and he was suddenly as cold as the snow. Rumpel-Stiltskin was gone. And so we buried him. Here, in this box."

Tom and the rest stood there, gazing at the gnome's coffin.

"But he wasn't out of time after all," Tom said.

"So it seems," said Anderlin. "He was given time. Or found time, somehow. In a way we can't understand."

"But Tom, he promised," Alexandra whispered.

"Promised what?" asked Anderlin.

Tom walked up to the coffin and stared at the name. "Rum said that if I helped him set things right, he would end my curse."

"What curse is that, child?" asked Maud.

"I bring terrible luck to everyone I meet," Tom said. He saw Maud and Anderlin's cloaked heads incline quizzically. "Except when my sister is next to me," he explained.

"I bring good luck," Alexandra said.

"It's a long, strange story," Conrad added.

Tom sighed. He put his hand on the lid, touching the

grooved letters. "I understand if you can't come back anymore, Rum. I hope what we did was enough."

Alexandra was right behind him. He felt her hand rest lightly on his shoulder. "It will be all right, Tom," she said. "So what if you can't break the curse? I'll stay with you. You won't be alone again. Not ever."

"OH, BUT THERE ARE WORSE FATES THAN LONELINESS!" screamed a coarse, cruel voice behind them all. Their heads whirled together toward the source. A small bearded figure limped out of the shadows at the edge of the lamplight. In the dim light, Tom might have thought it was Rum. But atop the head was not a broad, floppy hat but a crown studded with gaudy jewels.

"Stiltskin!" cried Tom.

"So, ye know part of my name . . . but not the rest, I bet ye!" Stiltskin said, and he cackled until the laughter disintegrated into a horrible, wet, hacking cough. He spat something gray and frothy onto the ground, and Tom was sure a tooth flew out with it. The gnome limped closer. One leg dragged behind him, and he wheezed and hissed with pain at every step. His arms were twisted, as if he had extra elbows in the wrong places, and both his quivering hands clung to a black staff.

"I see you cheated at your own game," Conrad said, stepping forward. "You never drank the poison, did you?"

"Oh, I drank it all right . . . been sick fer days. That poison kills feeble folk. But we gnomes are made of stouter stuff. Did ye not know that, ye fool?" The gnome spat again and raised the staff, leveling it at the group. Tom's skin twitched all over when he saw the carving of the horned creature on the staff's head.

"DO YE KNOW WHAT YE'VE COST ME, YE PACK OF IDJITS? All that gold, all that loot! And now ye're busy, undoing all the lovely suffering I caused! So now *ye* will be the ones to suffer, fer what ye've done," said the gnome with a growl. "ALL OF YE!" He raised the staff over his head and mumbled something under his labored breath. Tom saw reddish light flicker and grow in the jeweled eyes of the carved face.

Tom stepped in front of Alexandra. Then Conrad set himself in front of them both.

"Won't do any good," muttered Stiltskin. "If ye only knew what was coming!" His mouth contorted into an ugly, cracked grin, and it looked like the poison had eaten away at his gums and blackened his tongue.

"You don't even know how to use that," Anderlin said. Tom could hear a bristling, scratching sound as the quill-beast's hands crunched into fists. He thought he could hear another more ominous sound as well, as if hard rain had begun to splatter the entrance to the cavern and was moving toward them.

"Is that what you think, ye ugly hedgehog?" Stiltskin said, tightening his grip. "I heard yer idjit stories, all of them—even that nonsense about my fool brother's ghost! So ye think I haven't learned to wield this staff after all these years? I can use it better than ye know— and there are so many nasty, wicked curses I've learned. Perhaps ye'd like to be the first, Anderlin!"

"Stiltskin—look here!" called Maud.

Tom saw Maud reach up to push back her hood. "Don't watch," he whispered to Alexandra, and he turned his own eyes away. But Alexandra must have caught an accidental glimpse of the face, because she squealed and collapsed to the floor, where she curled into a ball and quivered with fear.

Stiltskin laughed at Maud. "Ha! Yer hideous face doesn't scare me!" He cackled so fiercely that his eyes briefly closed. Anderlin used the moment to spring at the gnome, reaching with his claws. Conrad followed, drawing his sword as he sprang.

In two steps Anderlin was upon the gnome. He leaped off his feet and soared through the air, unleashing his awful, otherworldly roar. Stiltskin opened his mouth wide and shrieked, just as the enormous form of the quill-beast obscured the tiny figure from Tom's view.

Anderlin landed on the spot like a great cat, spitting and slashing. Tom heard the screech of claw on stone. The quill-beast whirled right and left, swiping at the ground with such ferocity that Conrad had to leap back to keep from being flayed.

"Where is he?" Anderlin roared. "Where did he go?"

Wild, braying laughter echoed off the stone walls. The gnome was behind them now, perched on top of Rumpel-Stiltskin's coffin at the edge of the abyss. "Ha!" he cried. "Ye can't catch me as easy as that! No, it's time to pay for what ye've done—all of ye!"

Of course, Tom thought. *He can vanish, just like his brother.* His heart sank. For a moment he thought Anderlin had put an end to that sorry gnome's existence.

"Do ye hear it now? Do ye know what comes, bringing agony and death?" Stiltskin mumbled again. He pointed the staff toward the entrance and drew it back, as if beckoning something. Tom stared that way, but it was too dark to see what was making that noise. If it sounded like rain at first, now it was hail. Something, or rather a multitude of things, was coming at them, picking up speed. Tom heard Maud gasp. Whatever it was, she could see it with eyes that pierced the gloom. Tom looked again. And this time he saw it too.

It began as a few small flashes of something shiny and clear, like balls of glass bouncing out of the dark. And then more and more of them came, leaping and bounding, tiny crystal bodies propelled by powerful legs.

"Nippers!" cried Tom.

Stiltskin must have known Tom and the others were coming, and drawn the Nippers out of the swamp. There were more, thousands more, than Tom could have guessed. They surged like water from a shattered dam, jumping eye-high in a frothing wave, with bodies twinkling from the light of the lamps. Tom heard their shells clack against one another, and countless legs scrabbling on the stone.

The Nippers spread across the width of the cavern, cutting off all escape. Stiltskin flicked the end of the staff, directing them, and the Nippers poured around the coffin at his feet, forcing Tom and the others to back away. They were surrounded, with the wall of the cavern at their backs, the chasm to their right, and the horde of murderous insects gushing toward them.

"Halt!" cried Stiltskin, pointing at the Nippers with the staff. The torrent of tiny creatures slowed and settled into a wriggling, shiny carpet only a few strides away. Tom could see the nearest ones bend their long hind legs, ready to spring, while their wiry antennae quivered with antici-pation and their sharp mandibles pinched the air.

"Ow!" cried Alexandra. Tom saw her clap her hand on her neck, just as one of the Nippers hopped away and disappeared into the multitude. She checked her palm for blood. The skin on her neck was berry-stained, but still, Tom saw a red wound there.

"What, you thought the glumberries would save you?" shouted the gnome. "Not when the Nippers are under my spell!" He flicked the staff upward, and the entire glittering river of bugs reacted at once. Thousands of them leaped eye-high into the air in unison, and fell back in place as the gnome cackled.

"Let's see now," the gnome cried happily, singing the words. "Which of ye has caused me the most grief? Is it that ungrateful little witch who abandoned me the first chance she got?" He grinned at Alexandra, who stared fiercely back at him. "Or the fool who ordered the attack on my Marauders?" The diseased grin came to bear on Conrad before turning toward Tom. "Or better yet, the other redheaded rotter . . . Yes, he's the worst of the lot. IT WAS YER BAD LUCK THAT MADE ME

DRINK MY OWN POISON, WASN'T IT!"

Alexandra reached for Tom's hand and tried to pull Tom down beside her. Tom twisted away and stepped into the open.

"Good idea," Tom said aloud.

The gnome sneered at him. "What do ye mean, good idea? Are ye mad?"

"Could be," Tom said. "Come on. Let's play a game."

Stiltskin narrowed an eye. "A game? What kind of game, stupid boy?"

"You decide," Tom said. "What's your favorite game, Stiltskin?"

The gnome stared at him from the coffin top, with his lips curled into a sneer. "I know," he finally said. "I'll give ye a task. And if ye can't do it, ye'll all feel the sting of these Nippers, biting yer flesh until there's nothing left but the bones."

Tom couldn't help but shiver, remembering the keen pain that even a handful of those bites had caused him. But he nodded. "Fair enough, but if I can do it, you have to leave Londria forever and never come back. And you have to leave that staff behind."

The gnome chuckled. "Fine with me. But ye're sure to fail, stupid boy."

"What is the task?"

"Why," the gnome said, as his mouth curled into a horrible, corroded grin, "*ye have to guess my name. All of it, not jest the part ye know. In jest three tries!*"

"No, Tom," Conrad said hoarsely.

"Don't play this game, Tom," said Alexandra, weeping with fear.

Tom looked at her and smiled. "It's all right, Sister," he said, before silently mouthing two more words: "Stay back." He turned to Conrad. "No more strokes of luck, Father. It's time for the best man to win." Conrad looked like a tiger eager to spring, but he nodded.

Tom faced the gnome and clasped his hands behind his back.

"Is it *Roland*-Stiltskin?" he asked, taking a step closer to the gnome and the horde of Nippers.

"No," said the gnome. There had been a flicker of doubt on Stiltskin's face when Tom seemed so confident, but now the awful grin stretched wider.

Tom took a deep breath, held it for a moment, and guessed again. "Is it *Walter*-Stiltskin?" He took another step toward the gnome.

"*No*," the gnome answered with a growl. "And that's close enough!" He swept the end of the staff a bit closer to Tom. The river of Nippers bubbled forward. One of them bounded to the edge of Tom's foot, and he crushed it under his sole.

Stiltskin sneered and tightened his grip on the staff. His breath wheezed and rattled with moisture. His eyes narrowed to slits. "No more strokes of luck, indeed. Last guess, ye brat."

Tom paused. He cocked his head and listened carefully

to something nobody else could hear. When he was sure he'd heard it right, he nodded. "Well, then," he said. "I suppose your name must be *Zarwen*-Stiltskin!"

The gnome gasped, and staggered back as if he'd been struck in the chest by an arrow. "WHAT?" he cried. "WHAT? How did ye know? How *could* ye know? Wait—ye cheated! My brother told *her*, before he died!" The gnome pointed a crooked finger at Maud. "And she told ye! So it wasn't a guess at all! It was a cheat!"

"You're right, I didn't guess," Tom said. "But that's not how I know your name. I know because your brother told me."

"And how could he, if he's been dead for a year? And don't tell me his ghost told ye!"

Tom crossed his arms. "But that's just what happened. He told me just now. He's standing right next to me." Tom smiled at the ghost beside him. Rumpel-Stiltskin bowed his head in response. He looked different now— more gray and pale than ever. Tom could see right through his form, as if Rum was beginning to fade away. The gnome's voice was fainter as well, as if he was calling from a distance. Tom had to strain to hear what he was saying.

"HE ISN'T THERE!" snapped Zarwen. "YE'RE A LIAR!"

"It's true," Tom said. "He's right here. But I'm the only one who can see him."

"No," came Alexandra's voice, soft and filled with

wonder. Tom turned to look at her. "I see him now too," she said. "But just barely. He's right beside you. The little gray man in the pointy hat." She raised a trembling finger and pointed. Rum tipped his hat and winked at her, and she gasped.

"The children," whispered Maud. "Only the innocents can see!"

"I DON'T BELIEVE YE!" shrieked Zarwen.

"Your brother says he can make you believe it," Tom said, repeating what Rum called into his ear. "He says you should ask something only he could know."

Zarwen cackled nervously. "Oh really?" The staff shook in his hands. "Then ask yer ghost what was the name of our mother!"

Tom waited, listening. He smiled and shook his head. "Rum says that's a foolish question. You never knew your mother. And your wicked father wouldn't tell you her name. His name was Grozen, by the way."

Zarwen took one hand off the staff and crammed it into his mouth, silencing his own crazed laughter. He stared wildly at the empty air next to Tom.

"Rum says it was your father who ruined the both of you, feeding you nothing but hate and misery and bile," said Tom. "And he says it's time for you to let all that go. He understands what you're feeling now, Zarwen. He knows the pain you're in; it was the pain he felt, just before the end. Your arms and limbs ache, as if they're freezing and burning at the same time. You can feel your bones crackling inside you. And the more the pain grows, the more your hate grows. But you have to know that, after all these hundreds of years, the end is near. Your time is almost done."

"STOP!" cried Zarwen, prying the hand out of his mouth. The ghost leaned in closer, calling fervently into Tom's ear. Tom put up his hands but kept talking, and edged closer to Zarwen.

"Rum says, as bad as the pain in your arms and legs is, he knows the pain in your heart is worse. Because deep inside you know you've done nothing but evil all your life. You can say it isn't your fault, it's just the way your father raised you, but you know that isn't true. In your heart you always knew you could have turned away from evil. But you didn't. Neither did Rum, until the very end."

"Keep away." Zarwen moaned. His face contorted, and his good eye blinked madly while the frosted eye bulged. "I'm warning ye. . . ."

"Rum says don't wait another second. He says you can't make up for all the bad you've done—there was too much of it. But you can start. He lured you here to give you that chance. He knew you'd come to seek revenge. But he says you can find something else here: a new beginning. He wants you to surrender the staff, and leave—"

"NEVER!" bellowed Zarwen. Dark spittle flew from his mouth and caught in his beard. He wavered on top of the coffin. As the staff shook, the horde of Nippers shifted with it, surging back and forth, dangerously close.

"This is your chance," Tom said, raising his voice. He pressed his palms together. "Don't wait for death to set things right! Make this the end of evil."

Tom saw a change came over Zarwen's face, as if the truth was at last becoming clear. The jaw went slack and the eyes wrinkled at the corners. For a moment it seemed as if the evil was draining away and something else was taking hold there.

Then, just as quickly, the moment passed. Whatever struggle was taking place inside Zarwen's heart ended, and goodness died a quick, savage death. The gnome sneered. "LIES!" he cried. He swept the staff toward Tom, and the Nippers tumbled forth. "ENOUGH OF YER WICKED LIES!"

Tom edged back as the creatures came for him. He saw Conrad and Alexandra and the quill-beasts press their backs to the cavern wall, with nowhere else to go and the Nippers at the edge of their feet.

"Wait!" shouted Tom. Rum called into his ear, and Tom did what he was told, surely the last thing left to try. He pulled the strap of the All-key over his head and dangled the key in the air. "Don't you want this precious thing?"

Zarwen held the staff still, and his good eye glittered at the sight. "My brother's key! Oh yes, I want it. But I'll get it off yer bloody corpse!"

"Take it now," Tom cried. He hurled the key high in the air. "*Catch!*"

The key soared, swirling around the end of the cord. Zarwen bared his broken teeth and watched it fly over his head. It was too high to reach with his hand, so he raised the staff and stabbed it at the loop, snagging it. He opened his mouth for a triumphant cry, realizing too late what a terrible mistake he'd made.

The Nippers, still under the thrall of the staff, followed its command when Zarwen raised it over his own head. They bounded forth dutifully, all of them at once, swarming by the thousands as the gnome stood atop his brother's stone coffin. The attack was so swift and complete that Zarwen suddenly resembled a crystal knight, clad from head to foot in glassy armor. The Nippers were on his arms and legs and in his eyes and ears. They filled his open mouth and burrowed into his beard. With the key still looped around it, the staff slipped from his hands and fell, leaning against the coffin, still pointing up at Zarwen. *One more stroke of bad luck,* thought Tom.

Tom later wondered why Zarwen didn't simply vanish to escape. Perhaps whatever the trick required was made impossible by the ravenous swarm, or perhaps he was so panicked by the attack that he lost his wits. At first the gnome tried swiping the Nippers away. But as soon as he exposed a patch of red-pocked flesh, a dozen more bugs covered the spot. The gnome flailed his arms and swatted and clawed . . . and then became curiously calm. Tom watched, sickened and amazed, as Zarwen stood straight.

The gnome folded his arms, his oversized hands flat against his chest, as if they were the wings of a bird that chose to fly no more. He teetered backward, slowly at first. Then he toppled off Rumpel-Stiltskin's coffin and into the abyss, still enveloped by the glassy creatures. The rest of the Nippers followed, spilling like water over the brink until every last one was gone. And just when Tom thought this might be Zarwen's final ruse and the gnome would simply vanish as he fell, a sickening crunch echoed up from the depths of the chasm far below.

Tom looked at the others to make sure they were safe. And then he saw, dimly, the figure of Rumpel-Stiltskin. The little form with its twiggy arms and gnarly face was as insubstantial as mist and fading fast. Before he disappeared, never to be seen or heard from again, he said his final words. He looked like he was shouting, but the words came to Tom's ears as soft as a whisper.

"*Burn it, ye idjit.*"

Anderlin made a circle of stones on the ground outside of the house. Conrad built the fire, starting with
dried grass and twigs at first, and then adding sticks and
branches and logs as the blaze grew. Before long, there
was a crackling, popping bed of orange coals at the heart
of the fire, and flames twisted high into the air.

Tom looked at the black staff and the carving at its
head. The horned, wolfish face glared back at him.

"Now?" Tom asked.

"I suppose," Conrad replied, shrugging. "The fire's as
hot as it's going to get."

Tom stepped close to the blaze and held the staff out.
The heat singed his knuckles. He lobbed the staff onto
the fire, and it settled among the burning logs. He
stepped away and coughed into one hand from the
smoke. Alexandra took his other hand and squeezed it.

"Good luck," she said.

Tom smiled and squeezed back. "Right! Or no luck at
all, we hope."

"As for me," Conrad said, "I like a game of skill better
than a game of chance."

"Me too," Tom said. "Will you teach me chess?"

"Happy to," Conrad said.

Tom looked around at the others. The quill-beasts, Anderlin and Maud, nodded with their cloaked heads, and then turned to watch the fire.

At first the staff seemed to hardly burn at all. The flames licked at it, but it lay there, untouched. And then the black wood started to redden. The red brightened to a dazzling orange, and the heat of the fire grew unbearable. All of them put their hands before their faces and stepped back.

The light was so intense that Tom could barely look at it. He tried to peer through a narrow gap between his fingers. Something burst out of the fire. It looked like a ring made of both wind and light, spreading in every direction at once. It struck his chest, and he shut his eyes instinctively. Inside his closed lids he saw thousands of tiny sparks. The earth heaved under his feet. No—it was a great dizziness that made him reel, so strong that it was hard to tell which way was up. Alexandra's hand slipped out of his, and he heard a soft *thump* as she fell to the ground. Tom dropped to his knees, wobbled, and then his consciousness slipped away, as if his mind had decided to follow Zarwen-Stiltskin into the abyss.

When Tom finally pried his eyes open, it was nearly dark. The roaring fire was a sputtering heap of coals and ash. There was a blanket over him, pulled to his chin, and another tucked behind his head.

"Hello, Son," Gilbert Holly said.

Tom raised himself on his elbows. "Dad! How . . . how did you get here?"

"Conrad came and got me," Gilbert said. "Apparently the swamp is now free of Nippers."

"Everything went dark," Tom said. "When the staff burned. What happened?"

"The end of your curse, that's what happened," said Conrad, who walked up with a load of branches in his arms.

For a moment Tom felt lightheaded again, but it was a different sort of dizziness. "My curse is gone? Are you sure?"

Conrad dropped the branches onto the fire and dusted his hands off, smiling. "I'm sure, Tom. Look. Your dad's been by your side for hours now, and nothing bad has happened to him."

"It's gone, Tom," Gilbert said. "After all these years it's really gone."

It's gone. Tom repeated those wonderful words to himself, and started to laugh.

Conrad knelt by Tom's side and gave him a playful punch on the shoulder. "You laugh now, but it was scary for a moment. I thought I'd lost every one of you."

"Every one?" Tom asked, feeling a chill. He looked around and saw Alexandra sitting on the ground with a blanket around her shoulders. She waved. Then he saw something that made his breath catch in his throat. Where Maud and Anderlin had stood, there were two great heaps of quills on the ground and a pair of shredded cloaks, as if the beasts had simply disintegrated.

"No," Tom said. His stomach lurched, and he covered his mouth with his hand.

"It's all right, Tom," Conrad said, putting a hand on top of Tom's head and turning it. "It's better than all right. Look."

Tom saw a place deep in the Dark Dell, at the foot of a roaring waterfall. There, a man and woman stood by the cascade, partly hidden by mist. They were wrapped in blankets too, instead of clothes; his tucked around his waist, hers under her arms. The man had one of the woman's hands in his, and the other stroked the side of her face. They stared into each other's eyes.

"I thought the same thing you did at first," Conrad said. "That Anderlin and Maud were gone. But a moment later, the piles of quills stirred, and those two came crawling out, naked as babies. They were under a curse, just like you, Tom. A curse made with the same staff—only they never knew what it was that turned them into the quill-beasts. One of the gnomes must have done it to them. Probably because he couldn't stand the sight of two people so much in love. Anderlin and Maud lived inside those skins for twenty terrible years. And all the while they couldn't touch or even look at each other."

"You think that's bad?" called a voice Tom had never heard before. Tom saw yet another stranger coming out of the house. It was a portly, balding, round-faced fellow, wrapped in a blanket just like Anderlin and Maud. He had a bowl that was piled high with every kind of food that the quill-beasts kept in their kitchen, and he happily crammed bread and jam into his mouth. He chewed and swallowed loudly, and then said with a giddy grin on his face, "Try being a glow-toad for thirty years, eating nothing but moths!"

Tom stared at the fellow, slack-jawed. He looked at his sister, and she smiled, and the pair of them started to giggle, and then they fell onto their backs and roared with laughter until their ribs ached and tears streamed down their faces.

"Dark Dell, my foot. We'll need a better name for that handsome place," Conrad said as they waved good-bye to Anderlin and Maud. The loving pair, who couldn't seem to let go of each other's hands or stop gazing at each other's faces, had decided to stay in their oversized home in the narrow valley, at least for a while.

"Come and visit us again," Maud shouted from the other side of the swamp.

"Not for a couple of weeks, though," called Anderlin, pulling Maud closer.

"What did he mean by that?" Alexandra whispered as they walked away.

"I haven't the slightest notion," Tom said.

Soon they met Jordan and Rolf, who'd stayed with the horses outside the dell. Conrad introduced them to Hubbard, the man who'd been a glow-toad for more years than he cared to remember.

"It was that miserable Rumpel-Stiltskin who cursed me when he had the staff," Hubbard explained. "Caught me snooping around his abode. Which reminds me— we ought to make a stop there on the way back." And that was all he would say about it, although he would grin and widen his eyes whenever they asked why.

Tom rode with Gilbert, and Alexandra rode with Conrad, freeing a horse for Hubbard. Most of them rode quietly, smiling to themselves. But Jordan and Rolf chattered away, and Tom overheard part of their conversation.

"Do you know what makes me downright giddy?" asked Jordan.

"What?" said Rolf.

"The bit about the ghost."

"The ghost? Are you mad? That part makes my toes curl!"

"Think about it, Rolf. If there truly was a ghost, think about what that means."

"Which is . . . ?" Rolf asked suspiciously.

"Don't you see? Death scares us because we're afraid it means the end of everything. So we should all be so lucky as to see a ghost. Because that means the end isn't really the end at all. It proves that something comes after this mortal life—a spirit that carries on when our bodies cannot! That's a comforting thought if you ask me."

Tom turned his head and saw Rolf scratch the back of his neck, pondering the concept.

"No," Rolf said, shaking his head. "It still just makes my toes curl."

"Come on, come on," said Hubbard. They'd left their horses in the care of Jordan and Rolf and started climbing the hill, toward the chamber where Tom first found the glow-toad.

"Can't you tell us *why* we have to go back here?" asked Tom, following Hubbard up the ledge.

"We've had enough surprises, Hubbard," said Gilbert. He was next in line, holding Alexandra's hand. "Enough for a lifetime!"

Hubbard stopped and smiled back at the group. "One

more won't hurt," he said. He stood beside the entrance to Rumpel-Stiltskin's old home, in the cleft in the rock. "Come on in, Tom."

Tom sighed. He didn't want to enter this place when they'd come to collect the glumberries. And he didn't want to now. Just the thought of poor, wicked Rum, dwelling alone in that hole in the ground and marinating in his own misery for who knows how long, made his heart ache.

"Trust me, Tom," Hubbard said. "You think I want to go back in after living here as a fat toad for thirty years myself? But there's something here you really need to see." He ducked low and squeezed into the narrow passageway. Tom sighed and followed him.

The passage twisted right and left, and ended in the miserable chamber. Hubbard had brought a lamp, and so it was more illuminated now than Tom had seen it before. *Better lit, but still gloomy,* he thought, staring at the crumbling bed and chair.

Behind them, Conrad and Gilbert and Alexandra crowded into the tiny chamber.

"Notice anything, Tom?" Hubbard said.

"No," Tom replied. "Wait . . . yes!" He felt something scratch his chest. He reached inside his shirt and pulled the strap that held the All-key over his neck. He stared at the key. "It changed its shape again." And it had—it was longer than he'd yet seen it, with a single square prong at the end.

Hubbard grinned, and his eyebrows flicked up and down. He reached out and pushed the bed away from its spot against the wall, revealing a square door in the floor of the cave. It had an iron ring instead of a knob and a keyhole just below the ring.

"I may have been just a toad, but I still had eyes," Hubbard said. "Big, soggy round ones. Go on, Tom. Use the key."

Gilbert put a hand on Tom's shoulder. "Go ahead, Tom."

Tom put the key into the hole. It was a perfect fit, of course. It resisted at first when he tried to turn it, but finally, with a groan, something inside the ancient lock shifted and tumbled. Tom reached for the iron ring and pulled it, and the door swung upward with a rusty screech.

The light of the lamp fell on a flight of wooden stairs that disappeared into shadow.

"What's down there?" Tom asked.

"See for yourself. No sense ruining the surprise now!" Hubbard said happily, handing Tom the lantern.

Tom took the light. He put a foot on the first step, testing its strength. It seemed soft but sturdy, so he took the next steps with more confidence. The rotted wood of the fourth step collapsed under his weight, and the stairway broke in two. As he fell, he heard Hubbard cry out, and felt a hand clutch in vain at his arm.

The drop wasn't far. He landed in a crouch onto a

rounded heap of something, just a few feet below. Whatever was under him shifted slightly with the jingle and clink of metal. The lantern's light filled a chamber much bigger than the one above.

"Tom!" called Alexandra.

"Are you all right?" shouted Conrad.

"Oh my goodness," Tom said, as his eyes finally perceived what he'd fallen into. He dropped to his knees.

"What's down there?" Gilbert cried.

"Something worth its weight in gold," said Hubbard.

"What's that?" asked Conrad.

"Gold, of course!" crowed Hubbard.

The chamber was filled with loot, in a pile so deep Tom couldn't see the floor. He was kneeling on a hill of coins. As the golden pieces shifted and tumbled under his weight, jewels were exposed, glittering white and red and green. Tom raised the lamp and saw more, everywhere around him. The sea of coins was studded with candlesticks, goblets, bowls, vases, crowns, necklaces, bracelets, rings, gilded picture frames with the paintings torn crudely from the middle, statues, and even a bejeweled, half-buried throne.

"What do you think, Tom?" called down Hubbard. "Except for the gold he exchanged for straw, that's everything the gnome ever stole. And a gnome can steal a lot in three hundred years! He never cared to spend it, you know. . . . He wanted only to make folk miserable by taking it!"

"Oh my goodness," Tom said again. He stared at the incalculable wealth. "What will we do with all this?"

"A lot of goodness," said Alexandra, peering down through the open hatch.

That's right, Tom thought. Rum had realized, almost too late, that he'd lived a villain's life, and there were amends to be made. He could never quite leave his rascally ways behind, but he tried. Was it enough, Tom wondered, to defeat the Marauders and cure a handful of curses? After all, Rum had lived for so long. There was a lot of villainy to undo. Could such a rogue be fully redeemed?

"We'll do this for you too, Rum," Tom said aloud. He picked up a handful of coins and let them spill back onto the pile. "We'll use it for good. And maybe, when all this is spent, that will be enough to balance the scales for you. I hope it will. I really do."

As he stood on the mountain of gold, Tom recalled his lonesome home on his solitary island, a place he'd never have to live again. He thought about dear Joan Holly, waiting to embrace him when he returned from this adventure. He looked up and saw faces smiling down. There was Gilbert Holly, the good-hearted man who'd risked so much for the sake of an accursed son. There was the sister he'd found, and the brave new father in his life. He took a deep breath because it felt like his heart was doubling in size, again and again. *That's what the heart does,* he realized. When there were new people to love, it didn't divide itself into smaller shares. It simply grew, as big and strong as it needed to be.

And when Tom thought about all of that, he couldn't believe his fortune.